符号中国 SIGNS OF CHINA

四大名著

CHINA'S FOUR GREAT CLASSIC NOVELS

"符号中国"编写组 ◎ 编著

中央民族大学出版社
China Minzu University Press

图书在版编目（CIP）数据

四大名著：汉文、英文 /"符号中国"编写组编著 . —北京：
中央民族大学出版社，2024.9
（符号中国）
ISBN 978-7-5660-2300-1

Ⅰ.①四… Ⅱ.①符… Ⅲ.①章回小说－介绍－中国－
明清时代－汉、英 Ⅳ.① I207.41

中国国家版本馆 CIP 数据核字（2024）第 017514 号

符号中国：四大名著 CHINA'S FOUR GREAT CLASSIC NOVELS

编 著	"符号中国"编写组
策划编辑	沙 平
责任编辑	买买提江·艾山
英文编辑	邱 械
美术编辑	曹 娜 郑亚超 洪 涛
出版发行	中央民族大学出版社
	北京市海淀区中关村南大街 27 号　邮编：100081
	电话：（010）68472815（发行部）　传真：（010）68933757（发行部）
	（010）68932218（总编室）　　　　（010）68932447（办公室）
经 销 者	全国各地新华书店
印 刷 厂	北京兴星伟业印刷有限公司
开 本	787 mm×1092 mm 1/16　印张：9
字 数	125 千字
版 次	2024 年 9 月第 1 版　2024 年 9 月第 1 次印刷
书 号	ISBN 978-7-5660-2300-1
定 价	58.00 元

版权所有 侵权必究

"符号中国"丛书编委会

唐兰东　巴哈提　杨国华　孟靖朝　赵秀琴

本册编写者

徐　刚

前言 Preface

创作于明清之际的四部长篇小说——《三国演义》《水浒传》《西游记》《红楼梦》，被誉为"中国古典四大名著"。这几部作品经过时间的淘洗依然历久不衰，成为中国文学

Known as China's Four Great Classic Novels, *Romance of the Three Kingdoms, Water Margin, Journey to the West,* and *A Dream of Red Mansions,* were written in the Ming and Qing dynasties. Withstanding the test of time, these four masterpieces are considered to be the best classic works of literature ever written in China. These works are not only literarily and socially significant, but also have a profound influence on the ideology and value orientation of Chinese people.

中不可多得的经典著作。它们不仅具有极高的艺术价值，而且深刻地反映了中国人的思想观念和价值取向，具有非凡的文学成就和社会意义。

　　本书首先对四大名著的作者、成书过程和主要内容作了简单介绍，然后重点介绍四大名著的主要人物和故事特色。通过这些分析，本书向读者展示了中国古典四大名著的艺术魅力。

This book begins with the brief introduction to the authors, creation process, and main ideas of the Four Great Classic Novels. It then focuses on main characters and writing styles of the four masterpieces. Through these analyses, it aims to showcase the artistic charm of the Four Great Classic Novels to readers.

目录 Contents

《三国演义》
Romance of the Three Kingdoms 001

《三国演义》概述
Synopsis of Romance of the Three Kingdoms 002

群雄逐鹿
Feudal Lords Vying for the Throne 008

计谋之书
Book of Stratagems 030

《水浒传》
Water Margin 043

《水浒传》概述
Synopsis of Water Margin 044

梁山好汉的世界
The World of Liangshan Heroes 047

替天行道显豪情
Delivering Justice on Heaven's Behalf 057

《西游记》
Journey to the West 065

《西游记》概述
Synopsis of *Journey to the West* 066

西天路上取经人
Pilgrims on the Journey to the West 069

真幻一体 庄谐相融
Integrating Fantasy with Reality,
Solemnity with Humor.. 078

《红楼梦》
A Dream of Red Mansions 091

《红楼梦》概述
Synopsis of *A Dream of Red Mansions* 092

红楼众儿女
Characters in *A Dream of Red Mansions* 096

虚幻与现实
Illusion and Reality 107

《三国演义》
Romance of the Three Kingdoms

　　《三国演义》是中国第一部长篇章回体小说，凭借其思想内容和艺术方面的辉煌成就，成为中国文学史上一座重要的里程碑。它描写了从东汉末年黄巾起义到西晋初年三国统一一百多年间的历史风云。全书主要反映了三国时期（220—280）的政治军事斗争，书写了那个年代各类社会矛盾的渗透与转化，揭示了时代的动荡与黑暗、人民的疾苦与希望，并概括了这一时代的历史性巨变，塑造了一批叱咤风云的英雄人物。

As a milestone in the history of Chinese literature, *Romance of the Three Kingdoms* is the first Chinese novel with each chapter headed by a couplet giving the gist of its content. It is a historical novel set amidst more than hundred years of turmoil starting from the Yellow Turban Rebellion at the end of the Eastern Han Dynasty and ending with the reunification of the Three Kingdoms in the early Western Jin Dynasty, reflecting the political and military struggles as well as the penetration and transformation of various social contradictions during the Three Kingdoms era (220-280) of Chinese history. Dealing with people's hardships and hopes in a period of chaos and disorder, the book summarizes the monumental historic changes of this era, and portrays a group of heroic figures of the time.

> 《三国演义》概述

《三国演义》别名《三国志通俗演义》，作者是元末明初的罗贯中。《三国演义》属于世代积累型作品，即这一作品是在此前已有的相关史料和民间传说的基础上创作而成的。四大名著中的《水浒传》和《西游记》也属于这一类型。

> Synopsis of *Romance of the Three Kingdoms*

Romance of the Three Kingdoms is traditionally attributed to Luo Guanzhong, who lived in the late Yuan and the early Ming period. *Romance of the Three Kingdoms* is a work that was compiled and created based on existing historical records and folk tales. The other two masterpieces, *Water Margin* and *Journey*

- **罗贯中像**

罗贯中（约1330—约1400），元末明初著名小说家、戏曲家，中国章回体小说的鼻祖，是14世纪中国为数不多的伟大作家之一。

Portrait of Luo Guanzhong

Luo Guanzhong (approx.1330-approx.1400) is extolled as a well-known Chinese novelist, dramatist and the founder of chapter novel, that is, traditional Chinese novel with each chapter headed by a couplet giving the gist of its content. He is one of the few great writers of the 14th century.

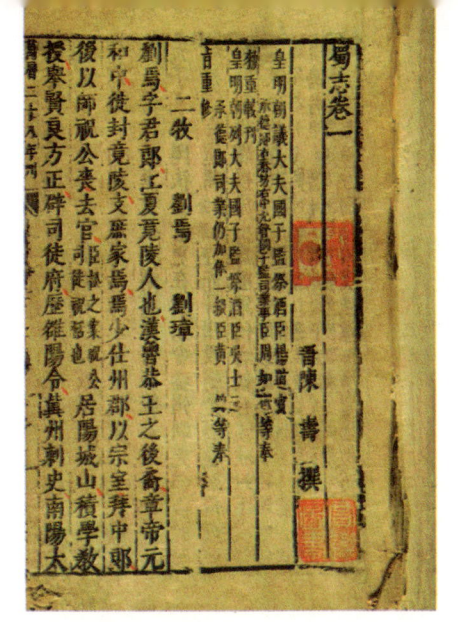

《三国志》书影
Photography of *Records of the Three Kingdoms*

早在罗贯中的《三国演义》问世之前，西晋（265—317）的陈寿便著有《三国志》一书，《三国志》是一部以记人为主、记事为辅的史书，《三国演义》的主要事件便是取自该书。到了南北朝时期（420—589），宋人裴松之为《三国志》作了注释，加入了很多奇闻逸事，从而为三国故事的广泛传播开辟了道路。宋元时期，许多三国故事成为说书人经常讲说的内容，这进一步促进了三国故事的传播。此后又不断有关于三国故事的文学作品诞生。正是有了前人的这些文学创作，

to the West, were also compiled through eras.

Records of the Three Kingdoms complied by Chen Shou of the Western Jin Dynasty (265-317) was prior to the advent of Luo Guanzhong's *Romance of the Three Kingdoms*. The major events in *Romance of the Three Kingdoms* were taken from this historical book, which was lied much in the vivid characters sketched in the novel. By the Southern and Northern dynasties (420-589), Pei Songzhi added lots of anecdotes and notes on *The Records of the Three Kingdoms*, thereby facilitating the popularity of the Three Kingdoms stories. These stories were often told by storytellers during the Song and Yuan dynasties (960-1368), which further contributed to their spreading. Since then, more stories related to the history of the Three Kingdoms appeared continually. It is based on these previous literary creations that Luo Guanzhong compiled *Romance of the Three Kingdoms*, the first Chinese chapter novel.

As the first chapter novel in the history of Chinese literature, *Romance of the Three Kingdoms* is among the most beloved works of literature exerting an ever expanding influence. The story

章回体小说

　　章回体小说是中国古代长篇小说的主要形式。章回体小说一般篇幅较长，动辄几十万上百万字。为了方便读者阅读，作者往往把长短大致相当的情节分成段，标上回数和题目，也就是所谓的分回标目。回目一般为简洁的对偶句，由人物、事件、地点以及与之有关的内容构成，如《三国演义》第一回的回目"宴桃园豪杰三结义 斩黄巾英雄首立功"。

The Style of Chapter Novel

As one of the main genre of the ancient Chinese novel, chapter novels usually have thousands or even millions of words. Authors tend to divide plots with similar length into different parts to be numbered and titled for the convenience of reading. Each chapter is titled by a couplet containing the main characters, events, locations and relevant contents. Taking *Romance of the Three Kingdoms* as an example, the title of Chapter 1 is "Three Heroes Swear Brotherhood in the Peach Garden; One Victory Shatters the Rebels in Battlegrounds".

• 《三国演义》插图
An Illustration of *Romance of the Three Kingdoms*

- 年画《战马超》

马超奉命攻打刘备的阵营,刘备命张飞出战。张飞与马超都是武艺精湛的猛将,交战百余回合没有分出胜负。刘备担心张飞有失,下令命他回营。张飞回营休息片刻之后,再次出战。又打斗了百余回合,仍旧没有分出胜负。这时天色已晚,他便命士兵点起火把与马超挑灯夜战。画面表现的就是两人酣战的场面。其中右边骑黑马的人是张飞,左边骑白马的人是马超,在他们两旁还各有一个挑灯笼的人。

New Year Picture *Zhang Fei Fighting with Ma Chao*

When Ma Chao was ordered to attack the camp of Liu Bei, Liu Bei sent Zhang Fei to confront him. Both of them were valiant generals. Neither of them won the battle after more than a hundred rounds of engagement. Apprehensive for Zhang Fei's safety, Liu Bei ordered him to return the camp. Having had a break, he returned to the battlefield again and fought with Ma Chao under the illumination of torches. This painting portrayed the fierce fighting between Zhang Fei and Ma Chao. The right one on a black horse was Zhang Fei and the left one on a white horse was Ma Chao. Two soldiers were carrying a lantern on each side of them.

罗贯中才得以将其加工、集合成中国第一部长篇章回体小说——《三国演义》。

作为中国第一部长篇章回体小说,《三国演义》也是中国流传最广、影响最深、成就最高的小说之一。其主要内容是:东汉末年,皇室衰微,各地起义不断。地处北方的曹操、西北的刘备和南方的孙权通过

happened in the final years of the Eastern Han Dynasty. The deterioration of the empire led to continual rebellions in every corner of the nation. Through continuous warfare, three major powers of Wei, Shu, and Wu were established, led respectively by Cao Cao in northern area, Liu Bei in northwest and Sun Quan in southern area. The history of the rise and fall of these three kingdoms is depicted in narrative

- 北京鬃人《三英战吕布》

《三英战吕布》讲述的是刘备、关羽、张飞三人大战吕布的故事。吕布英勇善战，一连斩杀了几员大将之后，各路诸侯都心生畏惧。这时刘备、关羽、张飞三兄弟主动应战，与吕布进行了一场酣畅淋漓的沙场血战，最终吕布战败，刘备、关羽、张飞三人声名大振。

Beijing Bristle Figures *The Three Brothers Fighting Against Lü Bu*

The Three Brothers Fight against Lü Bu tells a story in *Romance of the Three Kingdoms*. Liu Bei, Guan Yu and Zhang Fei were valorous enough to fight against courageous Lü Bu after several major generals were killed, which intimidated marquises. The reputation of the three brothers was greatly boosted after they defeated Lü Bu in this bloody battle.

不断的兼并战争，最终建立起魏、蜀、吴三大政权，形成了三足鼎立的局面。小说主要表现的就是魏、蜀、吴三国兴亡的历史。虽然《三国演义》以记叙历史为主，但在描绘大量的战争场面之外，还刻画了众多英雄人物形象。

小说文字浅显，人物形象刻画深刻，情节曲折，引人入胜，历史和文学意义俱佳，具有极其深远的社会影响。现在所见的《三国演义》刊本以明代嘉靖年间的版本最早，分二十四卷，二百四十则。清代毛宗岗父子又在此基础上做了一些修改，形成了现在最常见的一百二十回本。

style. In addition to battle scenes, a great number of heroic characters are portrayed in this novel.

The literary value of *Romance of the Three Kingdoms* lies much in the vivid characters sketched in the novel and the intricate plot written in simple but fascinating language; therefore, its influence has been profound and lasting in the history of Chinese literature. The earliest version was compiled during the reign of Emperor Jiajing of the Ming Dynasty (1522-1566), which was initially published in 24 volumes and 240 chapters. Mao Zonggang and his father of the Qing Dynasty edited the text, fitting it into 120 chapters, which has been the most common version so far.

北京鬃人

　　北京鬃人是北京特有的一种手工艺，距今有一百多年的历史。鬃人造型一般高十几厘米，用胶泥做头和底座，用秫秸做骨架，外绷彩纸（或绸缎）作为外衣，然后依据人物故事勾画脸谱、描绘服饰。因为在鬃人的底座上粘有一圈约二三厘米长的猪鬃，因此称之为"鬃人"。数个鬃人可以组成一组戏剧人物，玩耍时需要将鬃人放置于铜盘中，轻轻敲打铜盘的边缘，靠猪鬃的弹力盘中的人物便会舞动起来，再配上京剧的唱腔，就如同真人在舞台上演出，生动有趣。

Beijing Bristle Figures

The bristle figure is a unique handicraft of Beijing dating back more than 100 years of history. The figure is generally more than 10 centimeters tall, with framework made of broomcorn straws covered with colored paper (or silk) as its clothing. Its head and the holder are made of clay. Facial makeup and costumes are painted based on different characters in a story. Bristles in 2 or 3 centimeters long are pasted on the rim of the holder, hence its name. A few bristle figures can form a group. Taking advantage of the elastic property of bristles, a group of dramatic characters will dance if the edge of the copper holder is tapped. Accompanied on voices in Peking Opera, they can act as vivid as real persons' performance on the stage.

• 北京鬃人
Beijing Bristle Figures

> 群雄逐鹿

《三国演义》塑造了一批英雄形象，如刘备、诸葛亮、关羽、张飞、赵云、曹操、吕布、黄忠、庞统、孙权、司马懿……通过这些性格各异的人物形象，完整地勾勒出

● 刘备像
Portrait of Liu Bei

> Feudal Lords Vying for the Throne

Such figures with different characteristics as Liu Bei, Zhuge Liang, Guan Yu, Zhang Fei, Zhao Yun, Cao Cao, Lü Bu, Huang Zhong, Pang Tong, Sun Quan and Si Mayi in *Romance of the Three Kingdoms* are portrayed so vividly that a panorama of the history from the Three Kingdoms Period to the Eastern and Western Jin dynasties is unfolded colorfully. The writer reveals the conflict between Liu Bei and Cao Cao, being in favor of Liu Bei's action, focusing on his bloc and eulogizing its main characters, while making supreme effort to reprimand Cao Cao.

Liu Bei (161-223) was the emperor who established the Shu regime during the Three Kingdoms Period in Chinese history. As depicted in the novel, born

从三国到两晋这段波澜壮阔的历史画面。小说的作者在对三国人物的把握上表现出明显的"拥刘反曹"的倾向，即以刘备集团作为描写的中心，对刘备集团的主要人物加以歌颂，而对曹操的行为则极力揭露和鞭挞。

刘备（161—223），三国中蜀国的开国皇帝。小说中的刘备，出身颇不平凡，是汉景帝之子中山靖王刘胜的后代。他少年丧父，靠贩鞋、织草席为生。黄巾军起义爆发后，刘备曾因组建队伍镇压起义军而立下战功，被任命为县尉，但是不久后他便弃官。随后，各地诸侯纷纷割据，刘备也建立了自己的武装，但因势力弱小，经常寄人篱下。他先后投靠过很多人，但仍不能扩充自己的力量，情形十分狼狈。好在绝望之中，求得诸葛亮的辅佐，才得以逐渐壮大，最终在公元221年称帝，建立蜀汉政权。称帝之后的刘备，为了实现全国的统一，不断征战，最后在与吴国的交战中惨败，不久便病逝。

在《三国演义》中，刘备被塑造成一个仁君的形象。他为人谦

of extraordinary parents, he was a descendant of the Han royalty. His father passed away in his early youth. He was poor as a boy, and sold shoes and straw mats for a living. After Yellow Turban Rebellion broke out, Liu Bei was appointed as the county magistrate because of his exploit in suppressing the army of Yellow Turbans, but resigned shortly. During the time of independent regimes, Liu Bei built up his own armed forces, but his force was weak and he had to depend on others for living. He had sought refuge with others without obtaining his own territory after twists and turns. In despair, he sought assistance from Zhuge Liang, an outstanding statesman and strategist of the Three Kingdoms Period. Under his assistance, Liu Bei was proclaimed emperor in 221 A.D., and established the Shu-Han regime. Continual wars for his great cause of unification broke out. His troops suffered heavy losses in a battle with Wu. Shortly after that, he died of disease.

Liu Bei is portrayed as a benevolent emperor in *Romance of the Three Kingdoms*. He was humble, courteous, ambitious and apt at making good use of talents. As recorded in the book, when Liu Bei was defeated by Cao

- 《刘备招亲图》棒槌瓶（清）

"刘备招亲"讲述的是：刘备早年曾经借了吴国的荆州作为自己的立足之地。当他势力逐渐强大之后，吴国便派人来索要荆州，但是几次都没成功。后来吴国便定下计策，邀请刘备前去赴宴，想要趁机扣留他，让他交还荆州。谁料当刘备到达吴国之后，吴国君主孙权的母亲一眼相中刘备，并将其女儿嫁给了他。于是，刘备吴国一行，不但没有损失，还娶得美人归。

A Club-shaped Vase with Design of *Liu Bei Heading for Wu for Marriage* (Qing Dynasty)

Liu Bei borrowed Jingzhou from Wu as his foothold in early time. Later when he gained ground, he was asked to return Jingzhou several times but Wu failed to get it back. Finally, Wu decided to trap Liu Bei into coming to Wu so that he was detained in exchange for Jingzhou. When Liu Bei attended the banquet in honor of him, out of Sun Quan's (the founder of Wu) expectation, his mother took a fancy to Liu Bei and announced Liu Bei and her daughter's betrothal. In the end, Liu Bei not only remained safe and sound but also got a beauty.

和，礼贤下士，宽以待人，志向远大，知人善用。小说中写到，他在新野被曹操击败之后，准备撤往江夏，路经襄阳时，很多荆州老百姓投靠刘备。有人劝说刘备抛弃他们，轻骑前进。但刘备本着仁义的原则，不忍抛弃，等到达当阳时，竟有十余万民众跟随，辎重数千辆，日行十余里，最终拖慢了行军的进度而被曹军追击。刘备不惜吃了大败仗，也不愿放弃老百姓的行为，赢得了人心。

Cao in Xinye and retreated to Jiangxia, people at Xiangyang went to Liu Bei to seek refuge. Liu Bei was suggested to disregard them and go forward. However, he was so righteous that he could not turn the cold shoulder on the people. More than one thousand common people with several thousand carriages followed him. Only several kilometers could they move forward every day. Finally, Liu Bei was

黄巾起义

　　黄巾起义是东汉末年由巨鹿（今河北宁晋县）人张角等领导的一次大规模的反抗东汉王朝的农民起义。因起义军以黄巾裹头，史称"黄巾起义"。

　　起义军领袖以传道和治病为名，在农民中间宣扬教义，进行秘密活动。十余年间，徒众达数十万人，遍布中国北方大部分地区。184年，张角下令全国各地教徒于三月五日同时起义，但在预定起义日期的前一月，出现叛徒告密，起义时间因而被迫提前。不久，起义震动京师。东汉灵帝急忙调集各地精兵围剿，最后黄巾军在政府军和豪强地主武装的联合镇压下以失败告终。

Yellow Turban Rebellion

Yellow Turban Rebellion broke out at the end of Eastern Han Dynasty under the leadership of Zhang Jiao of Julu county (today's Ningjin county of Hebei Province). Rebels wore yellow turbans, hence its name.

　　The rebels proclaimed their doctrine among the peasants in the name of cure for disease and preaching. The number of the followers reached more than 100,000 spreading most areas of northern China in a decade of underground activities. In 184 A.D., Zhang Jiao ordered all his followers to stage an uprising on March 5th. Unfortunately, the uprising was forced to be earlier than the original schedule because a traitor let out the date of rebellion one month before it happened. Soon after, Emperor Lingdi of the Eastern Han Dynasty summoned his troops to crack down on it in no time. The rebellion was suppressed by imperial armies and strong landholder forces in the end.

• 黄巾起义
A Scene from Yellow Turban Rebellion

• 四川成都汉昭烈庙
Zhaolie Memorial Temple in Chengdu, Sichuan Province

小说中还写到，为了能够求得诸葛亮的辅佐，刘备曾经"三顾茅庐"，亲自去诸葛亮的家中请他。第一次去拜访时，恰巧诸葛亮不在家。第二次又去拜访时，他仍是不在。同去的关羽、张飞便觉得诸葛亮是徒有虚名，劝刘备不要再去拜访他了。但是刘备认定诸葛亮是一位贤能的人，便再次去拜访他。第三次去诸葛亮家时，诸葛亮正在

pursued and attacked by Cao Cao. He would rather suffer a deadly defeat than abandon the ordinary people. What he did won the common people's heart.

Liu Bei succeeded in recruiting Zhuge Liang after paying three personal visits to seek his assistance in the great cause of unification. As luck would have it, Zhuge Liang was away that day when Liu Bei, Guan Yu and Zhang Fei first time called on him. Zhuge Liang was also

午睡，为了不打扰他睡觉，刘备便站在门外等着他醒来。经过这样一番试探，诸葛亮觉得刘备是一位明君，便跟随刘备出山了，并在后来为蜀汉立下了不朽的功勋。

蜀国另一位重要的人物诸葛亮（181—234），在小说中被塑造为"千古良相"的典范。诸葛亮父母

not in during their second visit. Guan Yu and Zhang Fei suggested Liu Bei not to pay a visit again because they considered Zhuge Liang to have an undeserved reputation. However, Liu Bei didn't give it up because he was firmly convinced that Zhuge Liang was an intelligent and learned scholar. Zhuge Liang was napping at their third-time visit, and Liu

- 皮影《三顾茅庐》
Shadow Play of *Liu Bei Making Three Visits at Zhuge Liang's Thatched Cottage*

皮影

  皮影,又称"灯影",是一种以兽皮或纸板做成人物剪影,在灯光照射下隔布表演故事的民间戏剧形式。皮影表演所用的影人的材质一般为牛皮、羊皮或驴皮,经过泡制、刮薄、磨平、晾晒处理,形成半透明状,之后再用刻刀在皮子上进行镂刻。为使影人能活动自由,影人的头、胸、腰、手、腿及臀等部分需要分别制作,一般一幅皮影需要雕刻3000多刀才能完成。此外,还需要给刻好的影人涂抹上颜色。最后,为了便于操作这些影人,还须在各部分加上操纵杆。

Shadow Play

Shadow play is an ancient form of storytelling and entertainment. Shadow play figures are paper or hide cut-out figures which are held between a source of light and a translucent screen or scrim. Figures are mostly made of cowhide, sheepskin and donkey skin which are soaked, polished and dried to be translucent before they are hollow-out carved. Each part of the shadow puppet including head, chest, waist, hands, legs and buttocks has to be made separately so a complete shadow puppet has to be carved more than 3000 times. In addition, carved figures need to be colored. To create the impression of moving humans and other three-dimensional objects, each part is to be connected by joysticks.

- 皮影人物——关羽
Shadow Figure Guan Yu

早亡，由叔父抚养长大，后因社会动乱，便避乱荆州，潜心向学。刘备三次去他家邀请他出山，他才出来辅佐刘备。面对当时的局势，他提出联合东吴，建立孙刘联盟，共同对付曹操的战略，从而奠定了三国鼎立的基础。

小说中的诸葛亮是一位具有高超智谋的人，在他的精心谋划之下，蜀汉打了一次次的胜仗。火烧博望坡之战，是诸葛亮出山之后打的第一个胜仗。当时刘备刚刚建立自己的军队，军事实力远远不如曹操。而恰巧这时，曹操派大将夏侯

• 诸葛亮像
Portrait of Zhuge Liang

Bei waited outside in case of waking him up. After rounds of testing, Zhuge Liang decided that Liu Bei is a virtuous leader, and followed him. Since then, Zhuge Liang accomplished extraordinary feats for Liu Bei.

Zhuge Liang (181-234) was a prime minister of the state of Shu during the Three Kingdoms Period of Chinese history. He is often recognized as the greatest and most accomplished strategist of his era and was consequently set as an eternal example of a wise strategist in literature. Due to his parents' early death, he was brought up by his uncle. Later, he moved to Jingzhou to escape from the social upheaval. There, he made a living by cultivation and studying. Liu Bei came in person to Zhuge Liang's reclusive place several times to consult on the strategy, which became the well-known story of "Three visits at Zhuge Liang's thatched cottage". Touched by Liu's good faith and courtesy to the wise, he accepted Liu's invitation to assist him. It was a time when various political forces were fighting with one another to rule the whole country in ancient China. He put forward the strategy of taking Wu as his alliance to be jointly against Wei, therefore laying the foundation

《三国演义》绣像

The Tapestry Portrait of *Romance of the Three Kingdoms*

for forming the confronting situation of the three kingdoms.

According to the novel, Zhuge Liang is a genius with great strategy and wisdom. He led Shu troop in successive victorious battles. The battle in Bowangpo was the first victorious one after he joined Liu Bei. At that time when Liu Bei just organized his troop whose military might was far behind Cao Cao, one of Cao Cao's major generals, Xiahou Dun, led 100,000 armies to attack Liu Bei. Zhuge Liang was composed enough to face the outnumbered situation. He commanded Guan Yu and Zhang Fei to lead a group of soldiers and horses laying in ambush in the jungle for the enemy. A team of the old and handicaps following

惇率领十万大军杀过来。面对敌众我寡的形势，诸葛亮从容自若。他先命令关羽、张飞二人各领一队人马埋伏在山林之中。之后，便派遣赵云率领老弱残兵与夏侯惇交战，并佯装战败撤退，引诱夏侯惇进入关羽、张飞的埋伏之中。等夏侯惇领军经过山林处时，关羽、张飞两路便放火攻击。由于山路狭窄曲折，树木交杂，火势一发不可收拾，曹军死伤惨重。此外，诸葛亮还派遣一路人马潜入曹军后方，焚烧其军用物资，给曹军制造恐慌。当夏侯惇带领着残兵败将逃回之时，粮草也被烧光了。

　　后来，诸葛亮被封为蜀国的丞相，刘备临终时将自己的儿子托付给他，希望他能辅佐幼主完成统一中原的大业。为了完成刘备的遗愿，他先后五次进攻魏国，最后病死在陕西岐山五丈原。其"鞠躬尽力，死而后已"的高尚品格，千百年来一直为人们所敬仰和赞颂。

　　此外，蜀国大将关羽（160—220）也是作者重点刻画的正面形象。关羽，字云长，这位勇猛无比的武将，因其红面长须而被称为"美髯公"。东汉末年，他流亡于

a major general Zhao Yun fought against Wei troop and then withdrew to lure Xiahou Dun and his soldiers into the ambush. As soon as Xiahou Dun's troop went into the trap, they got fire attack set by Zhang Fei's troop and Guan Yu's troop from both directions. The the uncontrollable fire spread on the winding mountain roads caused heavy casualties of Cao Cao's army. In addition, another troop was sent by Zhuge Liang to burn the army provisions at the home front of Cao's army. When the defeated Xiahou

● 诸葛亮火烧博望坡
The Battle of Zhuge Liang Burning Bowangpo

- 四川成都武侯祠
Memorial Temple to Military Marquise Zhuge Liang in Chengdu, Sichuan Province

Dun fled back, all the supplies were burnt to the ground, which created panic among Cao's troop.

Zhuge Liang was appointed to the prime minister of Shu to exercise the military and political power. On his deathbed Liu Bei entrusted Zhuge Liang with his son. It was his last wish that Zhuge Liang could assist his young son to fulfill his great cause of unification. To carry out Liu Bei's last will, Zhuge Liang dedicated himself to conquering Wei five times in succession until he passed away in Wuzhangyuan, Qishan, Shaanxi Province. Zhuge Liang has been a respectable personage extolled by people in Chinese history.

Guan Yu (160-219), with courtesy name Yun Chang, a prominent general of the State of Shu during the Three Kingdoms Period, is another positive figure portrayed in the novel. History books have it that Guan Yu was brave and skillful in battles. Guan is traditionally portrayed as a red-faced warrior with a long, lush beard. He was named "Meiran

涿郡，结识了刘备、张飞二人，三人志同道合，便在桃园中结为兄弟。后来，关羽跟随刘备征战，忠心不贰，深受刘备信任。

小说中的关羽被塑造为"忠义"的化身，其中最能表现其忠义事迹的是他千里走单骑、过五关斩六将一节。关羽与刘备曾经一度失散，后来，关羽身陷曹操兵营之

诸葛连弩

　　诸葛连弩是诸葛亮发明的一种新式武器。它是在以往小型袖珍连弩的基础上加以改进的。诸葛连弩的弩臂上有一箭匣，可装许多支箭。同时还装有一个发射铁销，使用时只要连续扳动铁销，箭就可不断射出，大大提高了射速。虽然连弩的射程较近，但在骑兵快速冲击至近距离时，可于强弩之后、格斗兵器之前发挥快射作用，以增大杀伤力。

Zhuge Crossbow

Zhuge crossbow was invented by Zhuge Liang. It was improved based on the small-sized repeating crossbow. Zhuge crossbow is equipped with a case that can hold numerous arrows through an iron pin to shoot. It accelerated the speed of continuous shooting. While it does have a limited shoot range, it was good enough for cavalrymen to rush at a close distance to shoot. It was a high-powered weapon used prior to fighting weapons and after the regular crossbows.

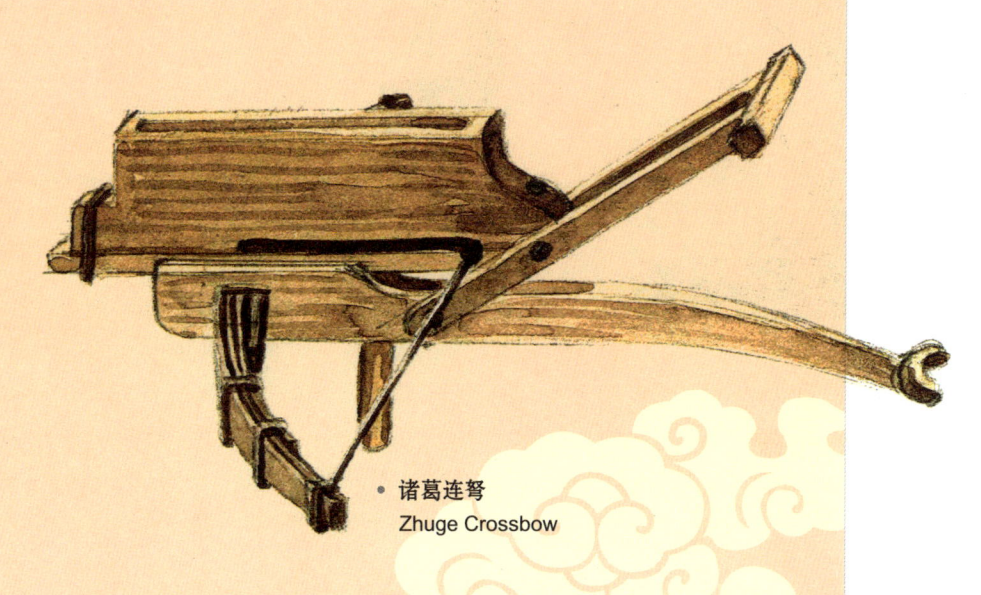

• 诸葛连弩
Zhuge Crossbow

• 桃园三结义
Three Heroes Swear Brotherhood

Gong" (handsome general with long beautiful beards). In the last years of Eastern Han Dynasty, he was in exile in Zhuojun and became acquainted with Liu Bei and Zhang Fei. The three heroes swore brotherhood in the Peach Garden. Guan Yu then followed Liu Bei into battles, showing unwavering loyalty that earned Liu Bei's trust.

Guan Yu is depicted as the incarnation of loyalty, which is embodied in the chapter of "Riding Alone for Thousands of Miles and Force Five Passes and Slay Six Captains". He once lost touch with his two brothers, Liu Bei and Zhang Fei and fell into the hands of Cao Cao, who wanted to take Guan Yu into his service. He offered official posts and wealth for Guan Yu, trying to win him over by any means; yet Guan Yu was not tempted. As soon as he heard of the whereabouts of Liu Bei, he left Cao Cao in no time. In order to obstruct him, Cao Cao deployed six great generals on the five passes of cites, but they were killed

中，做了曹操手下的一名将官。但是，当他得知刘备的下落之后，便立刻拜别曹操去投奔刘备。为了阻挠关羽，曹操在他途经的五个城关中设置了六名大将，但是他们都被关羽斩于马下，最后关羽终于回到了刘备营中。随后他为刘备立下赫

赫战功，一时间威震华夏。

关羽不但是忠义的化身，而且还有万夫不当之勇。他曾经"温酒斩华雄"。故事是这样的：各地诸侯讨伐董卓时，董卓手下的大将华

by Guan Yu one by one. Finally, Guan Yu reunited with Liu Bei. He afterwards achieved illustrious military exploits and became famous throughout China.

Guan is not only respected as an epitome of loyalty and righteousness but also full of valour and vigour. According

- **关羽使用的兵器——青龙偃月刀**

  相传铁匠在打造青龙偃月刀时失败了无数次，在炼到最后一炉火时，炉火中突然蹦出银白的毫光，斩杀了天上的青龙，青龙的血滴在刀上，才使得这把刀最终打造成功。

  Green Loong Crescent Blade, a Weapon Used by Guan Yu

  As the legend goes, a blacksmith failed to make a broadsword after numerous trials. Suddenly came out a beam of silver light and killed a green loong in the heaven. Speckled with the blood of the loong, this weapon was successfully built.

- **关羽的坐骑——赤兔马**

  赤兔马是古代的宝马，它浑身上下如鲜血般殷红，能日行千里，负重八百斤。渡江过河如履平地，在水中不吃草料，只食鱼鳖。

  Guan Yu's Red Horse

  The Red Horse is a kind of precious horse. It is blackish-red-colored all over. It can run a thousand kilometers a day. Loading 400 kilograms' goods, it can ford rivers as easy as running on the ground. It ate fish and turtles when it was in the river.

• 《关羽擒将图》商喜（明）
画作描述的是关羽活捉曹军大将庞德的故事。画中几近全裸的人是庞德，他怒睁双目，咆哮挣扎，两员大将将其按倒在地。而坐于石头之上的关羽则显得从容自若，他双手抱膝，美髯拂动，气宇轩昂，威武神勇。

Guan Yu Capturing a General, by Shangxi (Ming Dynasty)
This painting depicted the story of Guan Yu capturing Cao Cao's general, Pang De. In the painting, Pang De is nearly naked and glares furiously roaring and struggling with two generals who is trying to hold him down. Sitting on a stone, Guan Yu looks composed, mighty and valorous with hands over his knees and long lush beards swaying.

雄威猛无比，各路诸侯对其束手无策。此时关羽要求出战华雄。临上战场前，曹操倒了一杯热酒递给关羽，安抚他说："将军喝了这杯酒，

to the story, when the warlords formed a coalition force in campaign against Dong Zhuo, they could do nothing but nail-biting in combat with Hua Xiong, a brave general in Dong Zhou's army.

再前去杀敌。"关羽接过酒杯，放在桌上说："等我杀了华雄再回来喝吧！"说完，提着大刀上马而去。不多时关羽便提着华雄的头回来，此时杯中的酒还是温的。但关羽的性格中又有傲慢骄横的缺点，这也为他此后的大难埋下伏笔。他驻守荆州之时终因骄傲轻敌，不听诸葛亮忠告，而被东吴所破，致荆州失守。随后他败走麦城被东吴俘获，身首异处，令人扼腕，一代英

Guan Yu requested to fight with Hua Xiong, and Cao Cao poured a cup of hot wine to offer a comfort to him. Guan Yu left it on the table and said: "I will drink it up after I behead Hua Xiong." After Guan Yu defeated Hua Xiong and took his head back, the wine offered by Cao Cao was still warm. However, there is a negative side to his character; his arrogant foreshadowed his individual calamity. Because he underestimated the enemy and ignored the advice from Zhuge

关羽在中国民间的影响

关羽虽然只是三国时期蜀国的一位将领，但是由于历代文学作品对其神武和忠义形象的艺术化描述，使其深入人心。在他去世之后，先后有16位皇帝23次颁旨对其加封，且封号一个比一个高。公元1102年，宋徽宗第一个封关羽为"忠惠公"，此后历朝皇帝不断对他加封。到清光绪五年（1879），关羽的封号已被追加成"忠义神武灵佑仁勇威显护国保民精诚绥靖翊赞宣德关圣大帝"，他已经成为保佑万民的神。

在中国民间，人们称关羽为"关帝""关二爷""关公"，将其画像贴在门上，还在全国各地建关帝庙，以求他保佑平安。

• 门神关羽
Door-god Guan Yu

Guan Yu's Influence in Chinese Folk

Guan Yu was no more than a Shu general in the Three Kingdoms Period, Yet his true life stories have largely given way to fictionalized ones, mostly found in the historical novel *Romance of the Three Kingdoms* or passed down the generations, in which his deeds and moral qualities have been lionized. His anecdotes were told vividly and his loyalty and bravery were known to every household. After his death, sixteen emperors had granted more titles for him. What's more, among the twenty-three awards for Guan Yu, each following title was higher than its previous one. Emperor Huizong of the Song Dynasty in 1102 was the first to grant the title of "loyalty general" to him. Afterwards, emperors of later dynasties followed. During the reign of emperor Guangxu of the Qing Dynasty (1879), Guan Yu's title was granted as "The saint of force with loyalty, bravery, benevolence and faithfulness to protect the nation and the people". Apparently, Guan Yu has been symbolized as the protector of the people.

In Chinese folk tradition, he is regarded as "The Saint of Force" and "Lord Guan". People placed his portraits on their doors and built temples of Guan Yu across the country, hoping for his protection and blessings.

- 关帝庙
Memorial Temple of Lord Guan

雄也就此谢幕!

　　与对蜀汉人物的褒奖截然不同，对于曹操，作者持贬低的态度。

　　曹操（155—220）在《三国演义》中被塑造成一个"奸雄"的形象。他性格多疑、性情残暴、阴险狡诈。小说中写到，他睡觉时都怀揣宝剑，常常从梦中惊醒，起身后便砍死身边服侍的随从。有一次，他落难逃到朋友家中，朋友热情地款待了他。但是，他在离开朋友家之前，却将其家人全部杀害。究其原因，只是害怕朋友去官府告发他的下落，可见其残忍之甚。此外，

- 曹操像
Portrait of Cao Cao

Liang, he was defeated by Wu and lost Jingzhou. Afterwards, he was captured and executed in Maicheng.

In contrast to the positive depiction of figures of Shu, Cao Cao is portrayed with negative features in *Romance of the Three Kingdoms*.

Cao Cao (155-220) was titled Emperor Wu of Wei. In *Romance of the Three Kingdoms*, he is portrayed as a figure of treacherousness and brutality. The novel has it that he always fell into sleep with a sword in his hands. Awakened from a nightmare, he would get up and kill his servant. As another story goes that he was in distress and fled to his friend's place. His friend treated him hospitably but turned out to be killed by Cao Cao just in fear of his whereabouts being reported to the officials. What a cruel man he is! In addition, his character was tainted by being jealous of talents. In the novel, it is written that his counselor, Yang Xiu, often saw through Cao Cao's thoughts, and thus was soon executed by Cao Cao under false pretenses.

Despite often portrayed as a cruel and merciless tyrant, Cao Cao has also been praised as a brilliant ruler and military genius. Rising in the age of political

他还有嫉贤妒能的毛病。小说中写到，军中的谋士杨修屡屡能够识破他的心机，后来便被他找个借口置于死地了。

虽然如此，但曹操确实又是一个拥有雄才大略的人物。他崛起于乱世，扫荡群雄而一统中原。小说在一些重大战役中都突出地表现了他非凡的胆略与军事才干。官渡之战便是一个经典的例子。这是一场发生在曹操与袁绍之间的重要战役。曹操和袁绍都是北方重要的军事力量的首领。当时袁绍带领十万

and social chaos, he defeated several powerful warlord groups and unified the Central Plains. His miraculous victories showed his military talent and mettle, With the Battle of Guandu as an classic example. It was a crucial victory for Cao Cao in which he led a rebellion against Yuan Shao, who dominated the northern regions with powerful military forces, and led a troop of 100,000 to attack Cao Cao in Guandu. Two parties were at a stalemate for two months, leaving Cao Cao in a difficult circumstance. To break the stalemate, his counselor suggested to burn Yuan Shao's army provisions in

曹操与杨修的故事

杨修作为曹操的谋士总能参透曹操的心思。有一次，曹操命人建造一座花园，花园建成之后，他去视察。视察完毕，他便在花园的门上写了一个"活"字。当时很多人都不明白曹操为什么要这样做，便去请教杨修。杨修看到门上的"活"字，立刻明白了曹操的意思。他对众人说："'门'字加上一个'活'字，是'阔'字也。曹丞相是嫌此门太窄，要你们将门加宽。"于是，众人便按照杨修说的做了。后来，曹操见到花园的门变宽了，便问是谁的主意，有人告诉他是杨修，曹操便称赞了他一番。

又一次，有人进献给曹操一盒酥饼。曹操在酥饼盒上写了"一合酥"三个字之后便将其放在了桌子上。正巧杨修去曹操的房间，看到酥饼盒上的字后，便让房中的人都来吃酥饼。众人都不敢吃，杨修便解释说："曹丞相所写的'一合酥'就是一人一口啊。"因为在中国古代，字都是竖着写的，"一合酥"竖着念便是"一人一口酥"。众人在听了杨修的解释后才放心吃起来。

The Story of Cao Cao and Yang Xiu

Once, Cao Cao had the garden constructed. After his inspection, he wrote a Chinese character "活" on the door, which made many people confused. Because Yang Xiu, one of Cao Cao's counselors, often read Cao Cao's thoughts, they consulted Yang Xiu on this puzzle. When seeing it, he understood its meaning in no time. Door in Chinese character is "门". He wrote a character "活" on the door, forming a new Chinese character "阔" with the meaning of widening the door. Cao Cao learnt that it was Yang Xiu that read his thoughts and spoke highly of Yang Xiu.

There was another time when someone sent a present of a box of flaky pastries to Cao Cao, and Cao Cao wrote three characters "一合酥" on the box. Coincidentally, Yang Xiu entered into Cao Cao's room. Seeing it on the table, he asked everyone in the room to share it, but nobody dared to. Yang Xiu explained that Cao Cao has allowed everyone to take pastries, because the Chinese character written on the box can be read as "一人一口酥", meaning everyone taking a bit of flaky pastries. Upon hearing it, everyone started to enjoy the pastries.

- 《曹操赠袍》木雕

《曹操赠袍》讲述的是关羽归顺曹操之后，有一天，曹操发现关羽的战袍破了，便命人做了一件新的战袍给他。可是关羽却将新袍子穿在了里面，而将旧袍子套在了外面。曹操见此情景，劝说他不必这样节俭，关羽却说，他这样做是因为旧袍是大哥刘备赠送的，他不能喜新厌旧。听完关羽的一番话后，曹操更加敬佩关羽的为人。

Woodcarving of *Cao Cao Giving a Present of a Coat Armor to Guan Yu*

After Guan Yu claimed his allegiance to Cao Cao, one day Cao Cao noticed that Guan Yu's coat armor was broken, so he had a new one made and gave it to Guan Yu. However, Guan Yu wore his old one outside of the new one. Cao Cao tried to persuaded him not to be so thrifty, but Guan Yu said that the old coat armor was given by his sworn brother, Liu Bei, and he is not the person who abandoned the old for the new. Having heard what he said, Cao Cao admired him even more.

精兵进攻曹操，曹操在官渡迎战。双方僵持了两个月，久战不下，曹操的处境极为艰难。此时，袁绍从河北运来大批的粮草物资作为后援，屯于乌巢。曹操的谋士便向曹操献计，建议他偷袭乌巢，切断袁绍的粮草。于是曹操便亲自领兵率精锐部队连夜从小路奔向乌巢。当曹操的部队到达乌巢后，他便命人四处放火，将袁绍的粮草烧尽。听闻乌巢失守、粮草被焚，袁军人心涣散，不久便逃回了黄河以北。官渡之战充分体现了曹操随机应变的能力。也正是这次战役确立了曹操在北方的统治地位。

● 官渡之战
The Battle of Guandu

secret. Cao Cao personally led a troop of infantry heading to Wuchao to burn down Yuan Shao's army provisions. Hearing the news, Yuan Shao's troop fell into disarray and retreated to the north of the Yellow River. This resulted in Cao Cao becoming the military ruler of northern China.

《三国演义》主要人物表
Main Characters of *Romance of the Three Kingdoms*

魏国 The State of Wei	曹操、典韦、许褚、郭嘉、荀彧、张辽、乐进、徐晃、张郃 Cao Cao, Dian Wei, Xu Chu, Guo Jia, Xun Yu, Zhang Liao, Yue Jin, Xu Huang and Zhang He
蜀国 The State of Shu	刘备、诸葛亮、庞统、徐庶、关羽、张飞、赵云、马超、黄忠、魏延、孙乾、姜维 Liu Bei, Zhuge Liang, Pang Tong, Xu Shu, Guan Yu, Zhang Fei, Zhao Yun, Ma Chao, Huang Zhong, Wei Yan, Sun Qian and Jiang Wei
吴国 The State of Wu	孙权、周瑜、黄盖、鲁肃 Sun Quan, Zhou Yu, Huang Gai and Lu Su

> 计谋之书

《三国演义》是一部不折不扣的"计谋之书",其间各种计策、权术轮番上阵,令人惊心动魄。小说里面的诡计奇兵,令人应接不暇。

《三国演义》中最具特色的是"韬晦计"。所谓"韬晦计",就是隐藏才能,以待时机。《三国演义》第二十一回写到,汉献帝认刘备为皇叔之后,刘备为防曹操疑忌,便每日只在菜园中种菜,装作胸无大志的样子。有一次,曹操请他喝酒,在席间曹操问刘备当今天下谁是真正的英雄。刘备故意装作无知的样子,并列举了一些当时并不是英雄的人来搪塞。曹操说,当今天下可称为英雄者只有你和我两个人。刘备听后大惊失色,吓得汤

> Book of Stratagems

Various stratagems and political trickery were ingeniously and excitingly depicted in *Romance of the Three Kingdoms*, worthy of the name of "the book of stratagems".

One of the most distinctive stratagems in *Roman of the Three Kingdoms* is to conceal one's own talent before timing comes. As written in Chapter 21, for fear of Cao Cao's suspicion, Liu Bei did planting in the garden all day long, pretending to be unambitious, since the emperor Xian of Han Dynasty took Liu Bei as his royal uncle. One day, Cao Cao offered Liu Bei a drink and asked his opinions of the real heroes of today. Liu Bei beat around the bush and enumerated a number of persons who were not much of a hero. When Cao Cao replied that only you and I were real

• 《武侯高卧图》朱瞻基（明）

此图描绘了诸葛亮隐居时的形象。他敞胸露怀，头枕书匣，仰面躺在竹林之下，举止疏狂，怡然自乐。

Marquise Zhuge Liang Lying Comfortably in a Bamboo Forest, by Zhu Zhanji (Ming Dynasty)

The painting depicts a scene of Zhuge Liang living in seclusion. He was lying comfortably in a bamboo forest exposing his chest with a bookcase under his head.

匙和筷子都掉到了地上。恰逢当时雷声大作，刘备慌忙辩称自己是因为害怕雷声而失态，而实际上他是担心曹操看破他的心思。这里，刘备便运用了"韬晦计"避免了曹操的疑忌。

除了刘备之外，司马懿也曾经使用过韬晦之计。《三国演义》第一百零六回写到，曹操的孙子曹睿死后，他的养子曹芳年纪尚小，由辅政重

heroes, Liu Bei was so frightened that his chopsticks and spoon fell from his hands. Coincidentally, there was a loud thunder. Liu Bei argued that he was terrified at the thunder. This is a classic example of employing the stratagem to avoid Cao Cao's suspicion.

Sima Yi also used the similar stratagem. As noted in Chapter 106, after the death of Cao Cao's grandson Cao Rui, his adopted son Cao Fang was so

臣司马懿和大将军曹爽共同辅佐执政。而当时的司马懿因遭到曹爽的忌妒失去兵权,于是他就推脱自己有病,回家闲居,同时还命令自己的两个儿子也辞官回家。当曹爽派人刺探时,司马懿立即披头散发在家里装病,并故意装作耳聋打岔,还声丝气咽地说自己"死在旦夕"。曹爽在得知这一情况后,非常高兴,以为自己从此以后便可以高枕无忧了。但是此后不久,司马懿便趁着曹爽陪皇帝出城打猎之机,发动了军事政变,逼迫曹爽交出兵权,而后以专权谋反的罪名灭其全家及其党羽,由此一举夺取了军政大权。这也是"韬晦计"的典型案例。

• 司马懿像
Portrait of Sima Yi

young that he had to be assisted by Sima Yi, a senior minister, and Cao Shuang, a general, jointly to rule the state. Sima Yi quitted office under the pretext of illness after he lost military power due to the jealousy of Cao Shuang. He also asked both of his sons to resign. When Cao Shuang sent his subordinates to sound out, Sima Yi pretended to be on the verge of death and panted out. Hearing of the news, Cao Shuang was immensely relieved. Shortly afterward, Sima Yi seized the opportunity when Cao Shuang accompanied the emperor on a hunting trip to stage a military coup, forcing Cao Shuang to surrender his military power. Cao Shuang together with his family and his followers was executed as conspiracy. Finally, Sima Yi seized the political and military power, another classic example of the stratagem.

    The stratagem of sowing dissension among the enemies is another common stratagem in *Romance of the Three Kingdoms*. As recorded in Chapter 8, no one dared to fight against Dong Zhuo, who seized the state power, because he was assisted by a valiant general, Lü Bu. Seeing the fact that Dong Zhuo would lose his power without Lü Bu's assistance, Wang Yun tried to stir up the

- 粉彩"吕布戏貂蝉"梅花形盘灯（清）
  Famille Rose Porcelain Quincuncial-shaped Lamp with Design of *Lü Bu Playing with Diao Chan* (Qing Dyrasty)

除了"韬晦计"，《三国演义》中运用得比较多的还有"离间计"。所谓"离间计"，就是在敌人内部挑拨是非，引起纠纷，制造隔阂，破坏团结，使之反目为仇。例如，《三国演义》第八回写到，当时朝中重臣董卓把持朝政，无人敢言，主要是因为他手下有一员猛将吕布。如果失去了吕布，董卓将很快失势。王允看准了这一点，与此同时，还得知董卓和吕布皆有好色的弱点，于是便指使养女

hatred between them. Taking advantage of their lascivious nature, Wang Yun used his adopted beautiful daughter Diao Chan as a lure and betrothed her to Lü Bu. Diao Chan was then presented to Dong Zhuo in secret. So irritated was Lü Bu

中国古代的"四大美人"

貂蝉与西施、王昭君、杨贵妃一同被誉为中国古代的"四大美人"。

貂蝉，东汉时期司徒王允的养女，貌若天仙。当时朝政把持在董卓手中，为了报答养父的养育之恩，她便在王允的谋划下周旋于董卓与吕布之间，最后使两人反目成仇。之后，貂蝉成为吕布的妾室。吕布被曹操所杀后，貂蝉跟随吕布家眷前往许昌，从此不知所终。

西施，春秋时期的越国美女，才色兼备。当时越国被吴国打败，西施被越王献给吴王做妃子。为了帮助越王复国，她利用自己的美貌迷惑吴王，使得吴王溺情于声色，不理朝政。后来，吴国被越国所灭，但是西施却不知所终。

王昭君，西汉元帝时期的宫女，貌美如花。当时北方的匈奴人经常入侵北部边境，扰乱当地人的生活。为了安抚匈奴，汉元帝便将王昭君嫁给匈奴的首领。王昭君抵达匈奴后，为维护边境的安宁作出了巨大贡献。她去世后被厚葬于今内蒙古呼和浩特市南郊。

杨玉环，唐玄宗的妃子，又称杨贵妃。她天生丽质，并精通音律，擅长歌舞，深受宠爱。杨贵妃得宠后，其兄杨国忠仗势欺人，玩弄权术。后来，安史之乱爆发，唐玄宗携贵妃和大臣出逃，途中为稳定军心，被迫将杨贵妃赐死。

Four Beauties in Ancient China

Diao Chan, Xi Shi, Wang Zhaojun and Yang Yuhuan are known as the Four Beauties of ancient China.

Diao Chan, Wang Yun's adopted daughter during the Eastern Han Dynasty, was very beautiful. In order to express gratitude to Wang Yun for his upbringing, she circulated between Dong Zhuo and Lü Bu so that they turned against each other and became enemies. In the end, Diao Chan became Lü Bu's concubine. After Lü Bu was killed by Cao Cao, Diao Chan followed other family members headed for Xuchang. Since then there has been no news about her.

Xi Shi was a talented beauty in the Kingdom of Yue during the Spring and

● 貂蝉
Portrait of Diao Chan

● 西施
Portrait of Xi Shi

Autumn Period. The kingdom of Yue was defeated by the Kingdom of Wu. To revitalize the Kingdom of Yue, Xi Shi was sent to the Kingdom of Wu as the ruler's concubine. Since then, the Wu emperor indulged in her beauty and turned a deaf ear to political affairs. Finally, the Kingdom of Wu was destroyed, but there has been no news about Xi Shi ever since.

Wang Zhaojun was a beautiful maid during emperor Yuan of the Western Han Dynasty. In order to appease Xiongnu who often invaded the northern border, the emperor ordered Wang Zhaojun to marry the leader of Xiongnu. She made great contribution to the peace on border. After her death, she had an elaborate funeral in the southern suburbs of Hohhot, Inner Mongolia.

Yang Yuhuan, the concubine of emperor Xuanzong of the Tang Dynasty, was also known as Imperial Concubine Yang. She was an inborn beauty and proficient in melodies, singing and dancing, and was therefore adored by the emperor. After she came into power, her brother, Yang Guozhong, threw his weight about. When Anshi Rebellion broke out, the emperor fled with his ministers and his concubines. Yang Yuhuan was sentenced to death in order to stabilize the morale of the troops.

- 王昭君
Portrait of Wang Zhaojun

- 杨玉环
Portrait of Yang Yuhuan

• 京剧《群英会图》（清）

京剧《群英会》是一出以蒋干盗书、周瑜打黄盖、借东风等为主要情节的剧目。画面中的人物从左到右依次为：鲁肃、周瑜、诸葛亮。

Painting of Peking Opera *Gathering of Heroes in Three Kingdoms Era* (Qing Dynasty)

This Peking Opera includes a series of stories in the Three Kingdoms, such as Jiang Gan stealing the book, Zhou Yu beating his senior general Huang Guai and Zhuge Liang borrowing the east wind. The characters in the picture from left to right are Lu Su, Zhou Yu and Zhuge Liang in sequence.

貂蝉离间董卓、吕布两人。他先将貂蝉许婚给吕布，而后又暗中将她献给董卓。这样一来，貂蝉便在二人之间挑拨离间，激起吕布对董卓的仇恨，最终借吕布之手杀了董卓。

除了"离间计"之外，"反间计"的运用也是《三国演义》中的神来之笔。"反间计"也称"将计就计"，是指在明知敌方人员是间

that he killed Dong Zhuo.

In addition to "the tactic of driving a wedge among the enemy", the counterespionage is also a highlight in *Romance of the Three Kingdoms*. This counter-espionage strategy involves knowingly allowing enemy agents to continue their operations while using them to transmit false information, thereby trapping the enemy in one's own

谍后，仍旧利用敌方人员为我方传送假情报，从而使得敌方中我方圈套。例如在《三国演义》第四十五回，曹操与孙刘联军陷入僵持状态。此时曹操的谋士蒋干主动请缨，想凭借与周瑜旧日的友情，前去招降周瑜。曹操欣然应允。蒋干来到东吴，还未劝降，便被周瑜看破来意。周瑜以"故人"为名假装大醉，与蒋干同床共寝，并故意将事先伪造的曹军大将蔡瑁、张允通

scheme. Chapter 45 is a good example. When Cao Cao's troop and allied forces of Sun Quan and Liu Bei reached deadlock, Cao Cao's counselor Jiang Gan volunteered to head for the State of Wu. He wanted to take advantage of his friendship with Zhou Yu (a military strategist working under Sun Ce and his successor Sun Quan) to summon him to surrender. However, ahead of his arrival, Zhou Yu saw through his plot. He pretended to be drunk and slept with

- 赤壁之战
  Battle of Red Cliffs

三国赤壁古战场

　　赤壁位于长江中游南岸的湖北省赤壁市西北部,三国时期著名的赤壁之战就发生在此地。在赤壁山临江悬崖上刻有巨大的"赤壁"两个字,相传为周瑜所写。当年赤壁之战,孙刘联军火烧曹军战船,把江边崖壁都映得通红。周瑜把酒庆功,酒酣之余,提剑在崖壁上刻下"赤壁"二字。这两个字虽经风雨的侵蚀、惊涛骇浪的拍击,但字迹至今仍清晰完整。赤壁也是中国唯一尚存原貌的古战场遗址,吸引着古往今来的人们前往观瞻。

Battlefield of Red Cliffs

Red Cliffs is located in the southern bank of the middle reaches of the Yangtze River, northwest of Red Cliffs (Chibi) city, Hubei Province, where the well-known the Battle of Red Cliffs broke out during the Three Kingdoms Era. There are two huge Chinese characters "Red Cliffs" on the cliff facing the river. It is said that they were written by Zhou Yu. When allied forces of Sun Quan and Liu Bei burnt Cao Cao's fleet to the ground, cliffs by the river were ablaze with flame. Zhou Yu drank wine to celebrate the victory and carved two characters of Red Cliffs with his sword on the cliff. It looks legible as ever withstanding the erosion of waves and bad weather. It is the only ancient battlefield well-preserved today, which has attracted many visitors.

● 周瑜像
Portrait of Zhou Yu

吴的密函放在桌上，以便让蒋干偷走禀报曹操。曹操得信后大怒，立即以通敌罪为由斩杀了蔡、张二人。这样一来，周瑜便借曹操之手除掉了曹操军营中最熟悉水战的两员大将。

这只是"反间计"的第一部分，更为精彩的还在后面。小说第四十六回紧接着写了曹操又派蔡中、蔡和诈降东吴，说自己的兄长蔡瑁无辜被曹操所杀，由于记恨曹操故而投降东吴。周瑜知道这必定是诈降，但他并不点破，而是将计就计。他与老将黄盖合谋，先是黄盖故意顶撞周瑜而遭重罚，后派黄盖的好友阚泽向曹操献投降书，声称黄盖欲投降曹操。曹操本来半信半疑，但此时正好蔡中、蔡和二人也派人送来密报，说黄盖受刑后痛恨周瑜想投降曹操，曹操方才坚信不疑。于是，在一天夜里，黄盖借着东风，乘着满载火器和柴草的船只前去投降时，突然放火弃船，火烧曹营，导致曹军大败而逃，这就是著名的赤壁之战。

另外，《三国演义》精彩的计谋还有"疑兵计"，其中最为经典的便是"草船借箭"。当时，曹操

Jiang Gan in his room. His fabricated confidential letter of Cai Mao and Zhang Yun, two generals of Cao, for the State of Wu was deliberately placed on the table so that Jiang Gan could take it to Cao Cao. After reading the letter, Cao Cao was so furious about the betrayal of Cai and Zhang that he beheaded them right away. As a result, Zhou Yu got rid of two senior generals of Cao Cao who were familiar with battles on water.

Another fascinating story related to the tactic of counterespionage is told in Chapter 46. After Cao Cao executed Cai Mao wrongly, he sent Cai Mao's brothers Cai Zhong and Cai He to feign surrender to the State of Wu under the pretext of the death of their innocent brother. Meanwhile, Zhou Yu has seen through the plot and turned Cao Cao's trick against him. Zhou Yu and the Wu general Huan Gai conspired to defeat Cao Cao with counterplot. As their plot shown, Huang Gai got heavy penalties because he offended Zhou Yu with bad remarks. After that, Huang Gai's good friend Kan Ze delivered his surrender note to Cao Cao. Cao Cao was suspicious, until Cai Zhong and Cai He, who were spying on Wu, sent a secret letter, mentioning that Huang Gai attempted to betray Zhou Yu,

• 草船借箭
Borrowing Arrows with Thatched Boats

率领八十万大军想要征服东吴，于是东吴便和蜀国联手抗曹。周瑜智勇双全，很有才干，可是心胸狭窄。他非常妒忌诸葛亮，利用军中急需用箭的机会，令诸葛亮在十天的时间内赶造出十万支箭。谁承想诸葛亮答应只需三天便可以造出十万支箭，还愿立下军令状，如果到时候完不成任务，甘愿受罚。周瑜心想，三天时间是绝对制造不出十万支箭的，正好可以利用这个机会除掉诸葛亮。然而正当周瑜暗暗高兴之际，诸葛亮却想出了"草船借箭"的计谋。

诸葛亮利用大雾弥江之际，令二十只草船向曹营进发，每只船上三十人擂鼓呐喊。当时曹操不知虚

whom he hated because he was tortured. One night, riding a boat loaded with firewood, Huang Gai headed for Cao Cao's camp. Suddenly he abandoned the fired boat and fled, setting Cao Cao's fleet and troop on fire, which became a well-known battle, the Battle of Red Cliffs.

Anothe story of using brilliant tactic to create enemy's suspicion is the story of "borrowing arrows with thatched boats". Cao Cao led 800,000 armies to conquer the State of Wu, which resulted in formation of union between the State of Shu and the State of Wu. Zhou Yu was wise and brave yet narrow-minded and jealous of Zhuge Liang's talent. Under the circumstances of urgently needing arrows, he demanded Zhuge Liang to make 100,000 arrows in ten days. Out of his expectation, Zhuge Liang pledged to fulfill this task in three days, and was willing to accept punishment if he failed to complete the task on time. Zhou Yu didn't expect him to make so many arrows in such short time and was pleased that he could get rid of Zhuge Liang in this way. However, Zhuge Liang made it successfully by employing the tactic of "borrowing arrows with thatched boats".

Zhuge Liang had twenty thatched

实，唯恐中了埋伏，便令一万弓弩手放箭，诸葛亮靠草船获得十万支箭。等到他令各船上军士齐声叫曰："谢丞相箭！"曹操才明白过来，但早已追之不及，曹操懊悔不已。而等到诸葛亮用草船得来十万支箭摆在周瑜面前时，周瑜也被诸葛亮气得半死。

《三国演义》中最精彩的"疑兵计"莫过于"空城计"了。《三国演义》第九十五回写到，诸葛亮在一场战役中几乎将所有的兵力都调往了前线，导致后方空虚，而这个时候魏国大将司马懿乘机引十五万大军向诸葛亮的后方袭来。当时，诸葛亮身边只有两千多名士兵，众人听到司马懿带兵前来的消息都大惊失色。面对这一情况，诸葛亮充分利用司马懿谨慎多疑的性格特点，巧妙使用了"空城计"。他命令士兵把四个城门打开，每个城门之上派二十名士兵扮成百姓模样，洒水扫街。他自己则领着两个

boats sailed toward Cao Cao's camp behind a veil of heavy fog. There were thirty persons on each boat beating drums and shouting loudly. For fear of falling into an ambush, Cao Cao ordered 10,000 crossbowmen to shoot continuously. After Zhuge Liang "borrowed" 100,000 arrows, he had soldiers shout in unison, "thank you for lending us arrows". Not until then did Cao Cao realize that he was tricked. Not only Cao Cao but also Zhou Yu was irritated.

Nothing is more exciting than the story about "the stratagem of the empty city". As noted in Chapter 95, Zhuge Liang deployed almost all the troops to

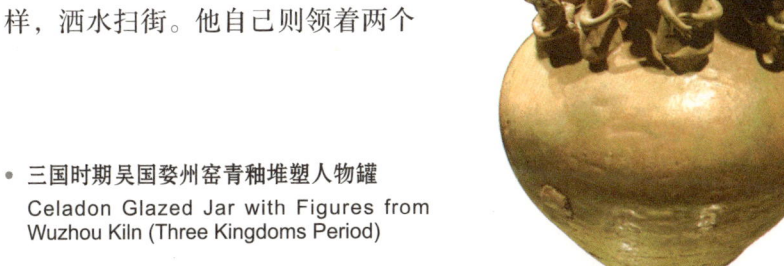

- 三国时期吴国婺州窑青釉堆塑人物罐
  Celadon Glazed Jar with Figures from Wuzhou Kiln (Three Kingdoms Period)

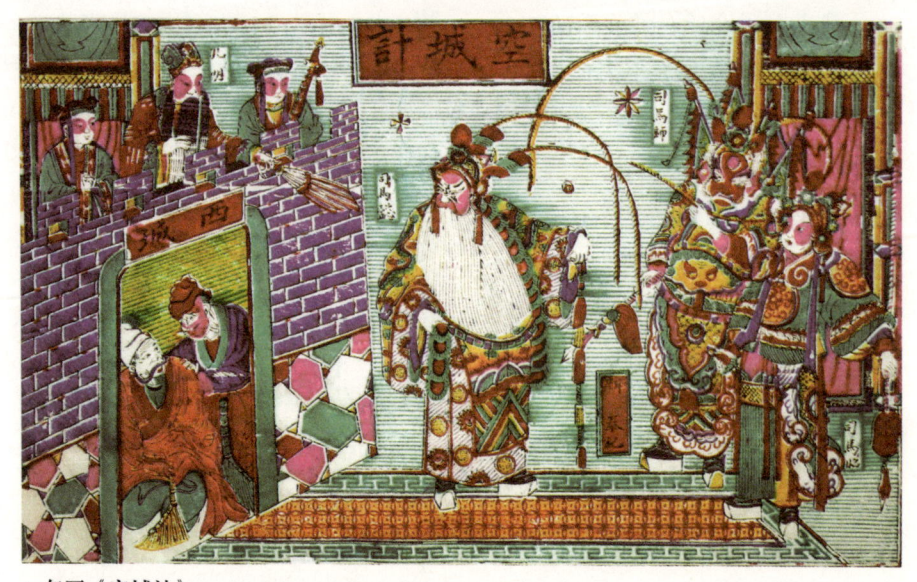

年画《空城计》
New Year Painting *The Stratagem of the Empty City*

小书童，带上一张琴，到城楼上弹起琴来。司马懿的队伍见到这种阵势后都不敢轻易入城。司马懿觉得诸葛亮一生谨慎，不曾冒险，现在城门大开，里面必有埋伏，魏军如果进去，正好中了他们的计，于是便带领各路兵马退了回去。诸葛亮有惊无险地保住了城池。

the battlefront when Sima Yi, a senior general of the Kingdom of Wei, led 150,000 troops to attack Shu from behind. However, there were only a little more than 2000 soldiers in the city to confront Sima Yi's main forces. Taking advantage of Sima Yi's suspicious nature, Zhuge Liang employed "the stratagem of the empty city", bluffing the enemy by opening the gates of a weakly defended city. Sima Yi was frightened to fall into an ambush and fled, thereby Zhuge Liang protected the city from being occupied by the enemy.

《水浒传》
Water Margin

　　《水浒传》是中国文学史上第一部史诗式地反映农民运动的伟大作品。在小说中,一百零八位聚义的兄弟以"忠义"相号召,他们替天行道,扶危济困,从落草到兴盛,从被招安到陨灭,谱写了一曲江湖儿女的慷慨悲歌。

As one of the four great classical novels of Chinese literature, *Water Margin* is the first to mirror a real peasant uprising in the history of Chinese literature. The novel depicts that one hundred and eight sworn brothers gathered at Mount Liang in the name of loyalty and brotherhood. From gathering to thriving, from being offered amnesty and enlistment to destroyed, the novel is soul-stirring and full of legendary stories.

> 《水浒传》概述

《水浒传》又称《忠义水浒传》，作者是元末明初的施耐庵。全书讲述了北宋末年以宋江为首的一百零八人在梁山泊聚义、除恶扬

> Synopsis of *Water Margin*

Water Margin is attributed to Shi Nai'an who lived around the end of the Yuan Dynasty and the beginning of the Ming Dynasty. The story, set at the end of the Northern Song Dynasty, is about how a group of 108 outlaws led by Song Jiang gathered on Mount Liang (or Liangshan Marsh) to spread goodness and punish evil-doers. The story of the uprising led by Song Jiang was a real historical event that lasted for three years from 1119 to

- **施耐庵像**

施耐庵，元末明初的小说家。他博古通今，才气横溢，早年他曾经为官，后弃官归里，闭门著述。他搜集整理关于梁山泊宋江等英雄人物的故事，最终写成《水浒传》。

Portrait of Shi Nai'an

Shi Nai'an was an official at his early age but he quitted office for literary works. As a knowledgeable and talented novelist at the end of the Yuan Dynasty and the beginning of the Ming Dynasty, Shi Nai'an gathered and compiled the stories related to Song Jiang and heroes at Mount Liang to complete *Water Margin*.

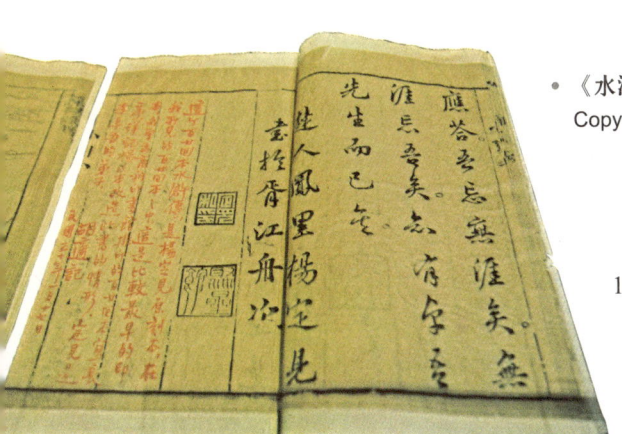

《水浒传》书影
Copy of Pages from *Water Margin*

1121 in the Northern Song Dynasty, and was recorded in the historical text. Even though the number of rebels was small, the insurgence led by Song Jiang posed a threat to the ruling class of the Northern Song Dynasty.

Similar to *Romance of the Three Kingdoms*, *Water Margin* is accumulated over time based on the related stories. Prior to the advent of *Romance of the Three Kingdoms*, some storytellers have begun to tell stories about Song Jiang and other heroes of Mount Liangshan. Their stories first appeared in *Old Incidents in the Xuanhe Period of the Great Song Dynasty,* which accorded with stories in *Water Margin*. Stories of Liangshan heroes were widespread because a large number of operas became popular in the Yuan Dynasty. Based on these materials, Shi Nai'an completed this celebrated classical masterpiece.

The novel vividly represents a grandiose social upheaval and victims of corruption and decadence in the North

善的故事。宋江起义是历史上确有记载的史实，宋代的史书中多有记载。起义的年代大约在北宋宣和元年（1119）至宣和三年（1121），前后三年多。这支起义军人数不多，但战斗力很强，在群众中影响甚大，曾经给北宋王朝的统治造成一定的威胁。

与《三国演义》的成书相类似，《水浒传》也属于世代积累型小说。早在《三国演义》问世之前，宋代就有说书人将宋江等人的故事作为说书的题材。现在所见到的最早描写水浒故事的作品是《大宋宣和遗事》，它所记载的水浒故事梗概和施耐庵的《水浒传》基本一致。元代大量的水浒戏的出现，也进一步促进了水浒故事的传播。施耐庵也正是在此基础之上，经过选择、加工、再创作，才写成这部优秀的古典文学名著《水浒传》。

小说主要描写的是北宋时期，朝政腐败，民不聊生，一群不堪忍受暴政的"好汉"揭竿而起，聚义在山东水泊梁山，竖起"替天行道"的大旗，劫富济贫，杀贪官恶霸。后来这些人又接受了朝廷的招安，平定了一些地方叛乱，最后主要首领被朝廷奸臣害死，一场轰轰烈烈的农民革命在悲剧中结束。

小说故事曲折、语言生动，塑造了宋江、吴用、李逵、武松、林冲、鲁智深等梁山英雄的形象，具有很高的艺术成就。现在所见的版本主要有一百回本、一百二十回本和七十回本三种。

Song Dynasty. A group of noble-minded outlaw heroes gathered in Liangshan Marsh to resist against unrighteous ruling in the name of justice. Song Jiang and his men later accepted the amnesty granted by the imperial court. Most heroes died in battlefields, and Song Jiang was also persecuted by treacherous court officials, thus a vigorous uprising came to a miserable end.

With lively, expressive language and intricate plots, characters with complicated personalities such as Song Jiang, Wu Yong, Li Kui, Wu Song, Lin Chong and Lu Zhishen were portrayed vividly. Currently, there are three common-seen versions of the novel, which are the 100-chapter edition, the 120-chapter edition and the 70-chapter edition.

> 梁山好汉的世界

《水浒传》里最为著名的人物无疑是梁山领袖宋江。宋江，面目黝黑，身材矮小，因在家中排行第三，对待父亲又十分孝敬，被呼作"孝义黑三郎"。他平日里爱习枪棒，好结交朋友。若朋友有难，他总会出手相救，故又被人称为"及时雨"。

宋江原本是县衙里的一个小官吏，因为妻子与人通奸，一怒之下，他便将其杀害。杀妻之后，他一直逃亡在外。在逃亡过程中，他结识了众多梁山好汉。但是宋江最终还是被官府捉拿，发配到江州城。由于在江州城得到好友照顾，他可以自由行动。有一天，他在江边浔阳楼饮酒，看到权奸当道、民不聊生，不由感慨万千，便醉题"反诗"于酒楼的墙壁上。这件事

> The World of Liangshan Heroes

Song Jiang was the leader of a group of outlaws who lived during the Song Dynasty. The short and swarthy Song Jiang had a reputation for being

• 宋江像
Portrait of Song Jiang

● **浔阳楼**（图片提供：全景正片）

浔阳楼位于江西省九江市，九江古称"浔阳"，故此得名"浔阳楼"。由于九江自古以来就是交通要道，所以位于江畔的浔阳楼历来也是名人云集之地。然而令其闻名天下的还是施耐庵《水浒传》中的宋江浔阳楼题反诗一事。

Xunyang Tower

Xunyang Tower is located in Jiujiang, Jiangxi Province which has been one of the main arteries of traffic since ancient times. A large number of poets visited Xunyang Tower and left their poems and inscriptions, but what made it widely known owes to the vivid description of the famous classical Chinese novel *Water Margin* (Shuihu) by Shi Nai'an.

被江州城的官员告发，宋江被判死罪。正当宋江要被执行死刑的时候，梁山好汉出现，将其救走，于是宋江便正式投奔梁山，落草为寇。走上梁山的宋江在众好汉的拥戴下被推举为梁山的首领。

宋江虽然上了梁山，但是不意味着他对朝廷的背叛。在他心中有着强烈的正统观念，希望自己有朝

extremely filial and generous in helping those in needs. As such, he earned the nicknames "Filial and Righteous Dark Third Son" and "Timely Rain".

Song Jiang was originally a magistrate's clerk in Yuncheng County. He escaped from Yuncheng County after he killed his wife who had an adulterous affair with his assistant but was finally arrested and banished to Jiangzhou.

《水浒传》场景雕塑（图片提供：FOTOE）
The water margin scene sculpture

一日可以归顺朝廷，为朝廷出力。经过多次与朝廷的沟通，最终梁山好汉被朝廷招安。但是朝廷招安他们的目的是以暴制暴，借梁山好汉去消灭其他的反叛力量。所以等他们将叛乱平定之后，朝廷便用毒酒将这些好汉毒死了。但即使朝廷赐下毒酒，宋江仍无半点怨言，顺从地接受了这种命运。

《水浒传》中的另一个重要人物是军师吴用，人称"智多星"，他与《三国演义》中的诸葛亮一

Thanks to his good friend's help, he was able to retain his liberty in Jiangzhou. One day, while drinking at Xunyang Tower, he thought of the corrupt officials in power and the people's suffering that he had seen, which moved him deeply. Inebriated, he wrote a poem inciting rebellion. An official in Jiangzhou discovered the poem and reported Song Jiang to the governor. He was arrested again and sentenced to death for allegedly plotting rebellion. Liangshan heroes stormed the execution ground and succeeded in rescuing Song Jiang from death. After that, he decided to take refuge in Liangshan, and he was held up as a leader of Liangshan marsh.

Even though Song Jiang had to join the Liangshan heroes, he didn't mean to betray the court from bottom of his heart. He held strongly to his faith in serving his nation with patriotism. Song Jiang's dream eventually came true after Emperor Huizong granted the outlaws amnesty. However, the real intention of the amnesty was to have them take down the other peasant insurrections. After

样，是一位极具聪明才智的人物。他有着卓越的军事指挥才能，在他的谋划之下，梁山队伍不断发展壮大。例如"智取生辰纲"一节：朝中的宰相蔡京过生日，大名府的梁世杰为了讨好蔡京，便准备了丰厚的寿礼，派武艺高强的杨志将其送到京城。为避免寿礼在路上被贼人劫持，杨志便与随从化装成商人的模样。晁盖、吴用、白胜等绿林英雄得知这批寿礼全是搜刮的民脂民

they quelled the rebellions, the surviving Liangshan heroes were poisoned to death with poisonous wine. Even so, Song Jiang accepted it obediently and submissively.

In addition to Song Jiang, Wu Yong is also an important character in the *Water Margin*. He was a brilliant military strategist nicknamed "Resourceful Star" for his wits, and was said to be comparable to Zhuge Liang. His expertise was vital in the rapid growth of Liangshan and the heroes relied heavily on him for battle plans. His wits can be seen in the chapter of robbing the convoy of birthday gifts of the imperial tutor Cai Jing. To curry favor with Cai Jing, Liang Shijie of Daming Palace assigned Yang Zhi to escort a convoy of birthday gifts. Knowing that these costly gifts were bought with money extorted from the common folks, a group of Liangshan heroes led by Chao Gai, Wu Yong, and Bai Sheng planned to rob the convoy. Yang Zhi and his men disguised themselves as ordinary traders so as not to arouse any suspicion from potential robbers. However, they still fell for Wu Yong's scheme at Yellow Soil Ridge.

Chao Gai and Wu Yong disguised themselves as date traders and Bai

• 吴用像
Portrait of Wu Yong

● 山东省泰安市东平罗贯中纪念馆智取生辰纲塑像（图片提供：FOTOE）
Illustration Statues Related to the Story of Robbing the Convoy of Birthday Gifts in Luo Guanzhong Memorial Hall, Tai'an, Shandong Province

膏，便打算将其劫下来。于是，等杨志一行人走到黄泥岗附近的时候，吴用便让几个人化装成贩枣的客商与杨志等人相遇。

当时正值中午，又是酷暑时节，众人饥渴难耐。此时由白胜化装成的一个卖酒的小贩正好由此走过，化装成贩枣客商的晁盖、吴用等人便抢上前去，围着一桶酒喝了个痛快。而杨志的随从也想去喝，但是杨志担心酒中有毒，便加以禁止。当看到那些客商喝完之后没

Sheng as a wine trader. The heat of that summer at noon was so insufferable, and the disguised date traders were gulping wine around the wine barrels. Seeing that they were safe and sound, the Yang Zhi's soldiers escorting the convoy joined them drinking, and drank another barrel of drugged wine. Soon all of them became unconscious. Once the escorts were knocked out, the Liangshan heroes made off with the gifts that were worth a large sum of money.

The story of Wu Song slaying the

事，杨志他们就放心地喝了另外一桶。谁料众人喝完不久，一个个都倒下了。原来，吴用趁众人忙着抢酒喝的时候，把一包蒙汗药放到了另外一桶酒中。因此他们个个没事，而杨志众人却都倒下了。于是，他们顺利地劫持了这批财物。

在《水浒传》诸多人物中，武松也是为人们熟知的一个人物，武松打虎的故事流传甚广。小说中的武松从小父母双亡，由哥哥武大抚

tiger is widely spread, making him known to most people. He was brought up by his elder brother after their parents died and has been away from home since his manhood. One day he missed his brother whom he hadn't seen for a long time and went to visit him. On his way home, Wu Song passed by a tavern where a large signboard reads "Three Bowls Do Not Cross Ridge". This aroused his interest and he stopped there for a break. The waiter refused to serve more after he finished three bowels of wine. He explained to Wu Song that the wine sold at the tavern was so strong that customers would become drunk after having three bowls and wouldn't be able to cross the ridge ahead, hence the sign. Wu Song remained sober after drinking three bowls thanks to his sound constitution. By the end of his meal, Wu Song consumed 18 bowls of wine in total and appeared tipsy.

He was about to leave when the waiter stopped him, warning

• 武松打虎
Wu Song Slaying the Tiger

养长大。武松成年后，一直行走江湖。有一年，他十分想念哥哥，便回家看望他。路经阳谷县，看到一个酒家的招牌上写着"三碗不过冈"，武松便走了进去。当他喝完三碗酒之后，店家便不再提供酒了。因为这种酒极好，一般人喝到第三碗的时候就已经醉倒了。但是武松自幼习武，身体强健，喝完之后并没有醉意。之后他又接连喝了十八碗。

当他起身要走时，店家又拦住了他，告诉他，前面的景阳冈上最近总有老虎出来伤人，建议他明天一早再赶路。但武松觉得自己有十八般武艺在身，便大摇大摆地朝景阳冈上走去。他走了一会儿，酒力发作，便迷迷糊糊地倒在一块青石上面大睡了起来。忽然武松感觉到一阵腥风扑面，原来是有老虎来了，便赶紧拿起身边的哨棒与猛虎搏斗了起来。那是一只体型巨大的猛虎，武松使出浑身的功夫与老虎搏斗，最终将其打死。

《水浒传》在塑造了一系列男性好汉形象之外，还刻画了一些女中豪杰的形象，如孙二娘、顾大嫂、扈三娘。

him about the presence of a fierce man-eating tiger at Jingyang Ridge. Confident with his excellent fighting skills, Wu song ignored the waiter and proceeded with his journey. While trying to take a nap to get over the effect of alcohol, he encountered the ferocious tiger. He picked up a staff to fend off the beast, and ended up slaying the beast by pinning it to the ground and bashing its head repeatedly with his bare fists.

In addition to male heroes, some female heroes were also portrayed in *Water Margin,* such as Sun Erniang, Gu Dasao and Hu Sanniang.

Water Margin described Sun Erniang as a fierce woman with a vicious and murderous look on her face. She had strong arms and legs that resembled clubs. She was well dressed and used heavy cosmetics, which made her resemble a yaksha and earned her the nickname "Female Yaksha". She was not good looking but highly skilled in martial arts. She and her husband used to run a tavern at Cross Slop. They lured unwary travelers into their tavern for drinks and knocked them out using drugs. They also made meat buns with human flesh fillings from their victims and served them to customers. When Wu Song passed by

• 年画《十字坡》（图片提供：FOTOE）
画面描绘的是武松手舞酒坛大闹孙二娘酒店的场景。武松一旁有孙二娘持刀、酒保端酒。

New Year Picture *Cross Slop*
This picture depicts a scene from the novel. Wu Song with a wine jar in his hand fought with Sun Erniang. Sun Erniang was holding a broadsword and the waiters are holding wine bottles.

孙二娘绰号"母夜叉"，从这个绰号上就可以看出，她是个比较凶狠的人物。《水浒传》中是这样描述她的外貌的："眉横杀气，眼露凶光。辘轴般蠢坌腰肢，棒槌似桑皮手脚。厚铺着一层腻粉，遮掩顽皮；浓搽就两晕胭脂，直侵乱发。红裙内斑斓裹肚，黄发边皎洁金钗。钏镯牢笼魔女臂，红衫照映夜叉精。"虽然她长相不佳，但却

Cross Slope, he stopped at the tavern for a break. But he was wary enough to see through Sun Erniang's designs. After speaking out their names respectively, they've heard so much about each other and became good friends. Later, when Wu Song tried to flee from calamity, he received help from Sun Erniang. He was disguised as a pilgrim by Sun Erniang so as to be free from misfortune. What she did was far more courageous than any

孙二娘开店
Sun Erniang's Tavern

other ordinary people.

Water Margin described Gu Dasao as having thick eyebrows, large eyes, a plump face and a thick waist. She wore several decorative ornaments on her head and wrists. When she was angry, she would beat up her husband. She was different from most women of her time, as she did not know how to do household chores like typical housewife. She earned herself the nickname "Female Tiger" for her fiery temper.

She was nicknamed "Ten Feet of

有一身好武艺，敢作敢为，体现出一种粗犷、豪爽的风采神韵。她曾经与丈夫在十字坡以卖人肉包子为生。武松路经此处时，孙二娘试图下毒药迷倒他，但是被武松识破。互相通报姓名之后发现是未曾见面的朋友，于是结下了深厚的友谊。后来武松落难逃到孙二娘这里，她巧妙地把武松化装成行者，从而为他免除了一场灾祸。在此过程中，孙二娘所表现出的对友人的关切和超人的胆识，正是平常女子所不能匹敌的。

扈三娘像
Portrait of Hu Sanniang

顾大嫂绰号"母大虫"，与孙二娘属于同一类型的人物。《水浒传》这样描写她："眉粗眼大，胖面肥腰。插一头异样钗环，露两个时兴钏镯。有时怒起，提井栏便打老公头；忽地心焦，拿石碓敲翻庄客腿。生来不会拈针线，正是山中母大虫。"她虽然长相粗俗但是为人豪爽，有胆有识。当她得知朋友被捕入狱时，便急忙找人商量营救；当有人提出只有劫牢的办法时，她马上称"我和你今夜便去"。她风风火火，为救人性命，将自己的安危置之度外。

扈三娘绰号"一丈青"。与孙二娘和顾大嫂不同，扈三娘可谓才貌双全，《水浒传》中这样描写她："霜刀把雄兵乱砍，玉纤将猛将生拿。天然美貌海棠花，一丈青当先出马。"她不但长相俊美，而且还有一身好武艺，手使一对双刀，勇猛无敌。

• 母大虫定计
"Female Tiger" Working out a Scheme

Blue". Unlike Sun Erniang and Gu Dasao, she was endowed with both beauty and talent. According to *Water Margin*, she was an expert in martial arts and wielded a pair of sabers. She carried a lasso as well, which she used to trip and pull enemies off their steeds.

> 替天行道显豪情

《水浒传》塑造的一群被逼上梁山的草莽英雄，他们担着与北宋朝廷作对的盗贼名号，却历来被人们称为"梁山好汉"。综观他们的精神品格及行为，可以概括出"好汉"的特征主要为：忠君孝亲、替天行道和仗义疏财。

"忠君孝亲"的思想贯穿在《水浒传》全书中。"忠君"是指忠于朝廷。宋江等人的起义虽然是对朝廷的公然反抗，但是他们起义的目的并不是夺取皇帝的江山，而是铲除那些欺压百姓的贪官污吏和土匪恶霸。小说中写道："宋江这伙，旗上大书'替天行道'，堂设'忠义'为名，不敢侵占州府，不肯扰害良民，单杀贪官污吏、谗佞之人，只是早望招安，愿于国家

> Delivering Justice on Heaven's Behalf

Water Margin portrayed a group of outlaw heroes who were driven to Mount Liangshan. Even though they resisted against the ruling class of the North Song Dynasty, they have been known as heroes because of their sense of justice, fraternity and their unflinching opposition to corruption.

Loyalty and filial piety run through the novel. Although Song Jiang and his men resisted the court, they didn't intend to wrest power from the emperor for themselves. What they did was no more than eradicating the corruptive officials, avaricious merchants and bandits that oppressed the common folks. As noted in the novel, under the banner of "Delivering Justice on Heaven's Behalf" and loyalism, they neither invaded local authorities nor caused havoc among

出力。"

梁山头领宋江始终念念不忘招安之事，并通过多种途径向朝廷示好，最后终于被朝廷认可。虽然朝

the general public. It was the corrupted official that they killed. They had always hoped for amnesty and to serve the country.

Song Jiang strongly advocated making peace with the government and seeking redress for the Liangshan heroes. These outlaws were eventually granted amnesty by Emperor Huizong, but the emperor recruited them just to root out them. Yet until the last minute of his life, as he was knowingly drinking the poisonous wine offered by the emperor, Song Jiang insisted, "I honor loyalty in my life. Even if the emperor punishes the innocent, my loyalty will not perish."

Filial piety is another characteristic seen among the

• 李逵像
Portrait of Li Kui

• 解珍、解宝双越狱（图片提供：FOTOE）
Xie Zhen and His Brother Xie Bao Were Rescued from the Jail

Liangshan heroes. Regardless of others' dissuasion, Song Jiang risked life to fetch his father at home. The moment he saw his father, his said that undutiful son Song Jiang made father worried. He also encouraged others to bring their families to Liangshan. Li Kui did so under his persuasion. Along the way, he encountered Li Gui, who impersonated Li Kui and robbed passersby in the woods in his name. Li Kui defeated Li Gui after a fight and wanted to kill the latter for discrediting him. However, after believing Li Gui's account that he had no choice but to rob to provide for his 90-year-old mother, Li Kui was moved and let Li Gui off. He even gave Li Gui some money and told him to take good care of his mother.

Confronting the corrupted ruling

廷征召他们是为了消灭他们，但是直到最后，宋江在喝下皇帝所赐的毒酒时，仍旧说："我为人一世，只主张'忠义'二字，不肯半点欺心。今日朝廷赐死无辜，宁可朝廷负我，我忠心不负朝廷。"

"孝亲"是指孝敬父母，这也是梁山好汉普遍具有的一种美德。

宋江上了梁山后，最为牵挂的便是家中的父亲。他不顾众人的劝说，冒着被捕的危险，回乡将父亲接到了山上。他见到父亲的第一句话便说："宋江做了不孝之子，负累了父亲吃惊受怕！"而且他还鼓励其他人将自己的家眷也都接过来。李逵便是听从宋江的劝说才下梁山回家接母亲的。路上李逵遇见了冒用他的名字做坏事的李鬼，依他以往的脾气，定会一斧子结果了李鬼的性命。但听李鬼说家中有九十岁的老母要赡养时，李逵便饶了他的性命，还送了银子给他做本钱。

梁山好汉的另一个重要特征是"替天行道"。北宋末期，朝政腐败，皇帝荒淫无道，百姓生灵涂炭。为了拯救人们于水火，梁山众好汉扶危济困，谱写了一曲正义之歌。例如小说"解珍解宝双越狱，孙立孙新大劫牢"一节，解珍、解宝兄弟二人本是登州城内的猎户，

class and the dissipated emperor, the grand assembly of the 108 righteous outlaws at Liangshan Marsh plundered and pillaged cities to save the people from untold miseries in the spirit of "Delivering Justice on Heaven's Behalf". As a story told in the novel, Xie Zhen and his younger brother Xie Bao were the best hunters in Dengzhou (present-day Shandong). Once, the magistrate

● 鲁智深像
Portrait of Lu Zhishen

因当地山中经常出现老虎伤人的事件，府衙限他们三日内捉住老虎。解珍、解宝两兄弟在山上埋下弓箭，射中一只老虎，不料老虎受伤后逃到了当地乡绅毛太公家的后花园里。解氏兄弟去讨要时，毛太公装作不知道，暗中把老虎交给了官府，又贿赂官府人员，要在狱中害死解氏兄弟。多亏顾大嫂等人相救，他们兄弟两人才逃出

sent them to hunt a ferocious tiger within three days. The brothers tracked down the tiger and arrowed at it. The wounded tiger hid in the backyard of Squire Mao's residence. The brothers went to claim the tiger, but Mao has already sent his servants to bring the dead tiger to the magistrate to claim his reward. He bought over the officials to imprison brothers and kill them. Squire Mao bribed the magistrate to sentence the brothers to death. Gu Dasao and others righteous outlaws raided the prison and succeeded in rescuing the Xie brothers. They killed Squire Mao and his family for revenge and fled to Liangshan Marsh to join the Liangshan heroes there.

In addition to loyalty and filial piety as well as the spirit of "Delivering Justice on Heaven's Behalf", chivalrousness is also depicted in *Water Margin*. Lu Zhishen is one of the lead character in the first part of the novel, in which he comes to epitomize loyalty, strength, justice but also brashness. Lu Zhishen's original name was Lu Da. He was first introduced as a garrison major. Having committed murder, he sought shelter in Wenshu Temple and became a monk, the abbot gave him the Buddhist name Zhishen, which meant "sagacious". As mentioned

• 鲁提辖拳打镇关西
Lu Da Beating up "Lord of the West"

狱去。出狱后他们诛杀毛太公，投奔了水泊梁山。

除了"忠君孝亲"和"替天行道"之外，《水浒传》中的好汉还体现了传统侠义精神所要求的"路见不平，拔刀相助"的品质。在众多的"以义气相称"的水浒好汉中，最得"侠"之精髓的要算鲁智深了。鲁智深原名鲁达，原本是一名下级军官，后来因为杀了人，被迫出家为僧，法号智深。"鲁提辖拳打镇关西"一节写到，有一天，军官鲁智深去酒楼上吃饭，听到了一对父女啼哭的声音，他便上前去询问原因。原来这对父女是受到了当地一个姓郑的屠户的欺凌。鲁智深见此情景，怒火中烧，当即便要去找他算账。他见这对父女无所依靠，先给了他们一些银子，将其护送回家，之后便直奔郑屠户的猪肉摊去。这个郑屠户在当地横行霸道，当地人都很害怕他，称他为"镇关西"。鲁智深见到他后，先把他戏耍一番，之后便与他打在了一起，最后三拳将其打死。

武松醉打蒋门神也是一例。武松由于杀人被发配到孟州监狱。在

● 武松醉打蒋门神
Drunken Wu Song Beating up Jiang Zhong

in the novel, one day while he was having dinner in an inn, he heard a singer crying over her plight. Having learnt that she has been bullied by a butcher nicknamed "Lord of the West" for bullying the local people, Lu Da gave her some money to help her and her father return home. He then went to confront the butcher, and killed him with three punches to the head.

Another example is the story of Wu Song. Because Wu Song committed murder, the court exiled him to a prison

梁山泊

　　梁山泊是小说《水浒传》故事的发生地，它位于山东省梁山县东南。梁山地处黄河下游，梁山泊形成于五代，古称"泽国"。唐宋不少文学家曾在此饮酒赋诗，至宋代，形成以梁山为中心的八百里水泊。如今，八百里水面早已退缩，留给今人的是梁山泊的遗迹东平湖。

Mount Liang

Mount Liang is well known as the stronghold of the 108 legendary Song Dynasty heroes of *Water Margin*. It is located in the southeastern Liangshan County, Shandong Province, in the lower reaches of the Yellow River. The area was from prehistoric times surrounded by the largest marshland in north China, called the Kingdom of Marsh, and later the Liangshan Marsh. During the Tang and Song dynasties, it was a place for many poets drinking and composing poems. Today, the view of "eight hundred li (Chinese unit of length 1 li equals to 500 meters) moorage of Mount Liang" cannot be seen any more. The relatively small Dongping Lake is what remains of the great marshes.

• 鼻烟壶内画《梁山好汉》
Heroes of the Water Margin
Painted in a Snuff Bottle

这里，他结识了施恩。施恩在附近的快活林开有一家酒店。后来有一个名叫蒋忠，绰号蒋门神的人霸占了这家店，还对施恩拳打脚踢。施恩一直敢怒不敢言。武松来到孟州监狱后，施恩便央求武松替他打抱不平。武松闻听此事，心中大怒。第二天便去找蒋门神。他以蒋门神所卖的酒水不好为由，先激怒他，之后便与他交上了手，最后打得他跪地求饶。

in Mengzhou. In Mengzhou prison, Wu Song befriended the chief warden's son Shi En. Shi En owned a restaurant called the Delightful Forest, but has been forcefully taken by a hooligan called Jiang Zhong, who was nicknamed "the Door Dod Jiang" for his fighting skills. Having heard what happened to Shi En, Wu Song was furious. The next day, he went to Jiang and found fault with the wine that he bought in the Delightful Forest restaurant in order to irritate Jiang. Wu Song ended up defeating him in a fight, and had him kneeled down to plead for mercy, successfully helping Shi En take back his restaurant.

《西游记》
Journey to the West

在四大名著中，《西游记》是最富有大众化特征的作品。它自问世以来，一直深受人们的喜爱。《西游记》之所以有这种艺术魅力，得益于小说中云谲波诡的幻想故事和幽默诙谐的游戏笔墨。作者吴承恩凭借其天才的艺术创造，充分驰骋其浪漫主义的奇思妙想，把读者引向远离尘俗的神魔世界，描述了一个个令人捧腹的故事，既为读者提供了娱乐和享受，又包含着无尽的教益。

Journey to the West is the most popular among the Four Great Classic Novels and has been loved by people since it published. The charm of *Journey to the West* lies in its engrossing and unpredictable stories, as well as its humorous and playful language. The author, Wu Cheng'en, used his genius artistic creativity to fully unleash his romantic and imaginative ideas, leading readers into a supernatural world far removed from mundane life. He crafted hilarious tales that not only entertain readers but also offer endless lessons.

> 《西游记》概述

《西游记》的作者是明朝的吴承恩。小说主要讲述的是唐代高僧玄奘带领他的三个弟子——孙悟空、猪八戒和沙和尚前往西天求取真经的故事。在中国历史上确有玄

> Synopsis of *Journey to the West*

Journey to the West is attributed to Wu Cheng'en of the Ming dynasty. It is a fictionalized account of the legends around the Buddhist monk Xuanzang's pilgrimage to the West during the Tang Dynasty in order to obtain Buddhist

- **吴承恩像**

吴承恩（约1500—1582），明代小说家。他早年不得志，直到四十岁才获得了一个小官职，后来因受人诬告，辞官回家，晚年以卖文为生。吴承恩自幼喜欢读野史趣闻，熟悉古代神话和民间故事。坎坷的人生经历使他对社会有了更深的认识，促使他运用小说的形式来表达内心的不满和愤懑，《西游记》便是这样一部饱含讽世寓意的文学杰作。

Statue of Wu Cheng'en

Wu Cheng'en (approx. 1500-1582) was a novelist of the Ming Dynasty. He did not have a low-ranking post until middle age but he did not enjoy his work, and eventually resigned, spending the rest of his life writing stories and poems in his hometown. As a child, Wu acquired the enthusiasm for literature including classical literature, popular stories and anecdotes. He was also familiar with ancient myths and folktales. Dissatisfied with the political climate of the time, focusing on the expression of emotions, he completed *Journey to the West*.

- 《西游记》绣像
  The Tapestry Portrait of *Journey to the West*

sutras, with three protectors in the form of disciples, namely Sun Wukong, Zhu Bajie and Sha Wujing. Xuanzang was a real Buddhist monk who was sent to the West to obtain Buddhist sutras during the reign of Emperor Taizong (627-649) of the Tang Dynasty. After his trip, *Great Tang Records on the Western Regions* was compiled from his experiences by his disciples. This book has preserved the records of political and social aspects of the lands that Xuanzang visited. The biography of Xuanzang was written by his disciples Huili and Yancong, Who added more mythological stories to this book. From then on, the story of the Tang Buddhist monk's search for the scriptures has spread far and wide. Based on the vernacular folklore of the Song and Tang dynasties as well as traditional opera, Wu Cheng'en accomplished a monumental literary work through great efforts.

The novel has 100 chapters. The beginning 7 chapters mainly described

奘此人，他曾经在唐代贞观年间前去印度求取佛经。后来，此次取经的经历被其弟子辑录成《大唐西域记》一书。这部书主要讲述了取经路上所见各国的历史、地理及交通情况，故事性不强。再后来，他的弟子慧立、彦惊撰写了《大唐大慈恩寺三藏法师传》，才给玄奘的经历增添了许多神话色彩。从此，唐僧取经的故事便开始在民间广为流传。吴承恩也正是在民间传说和话

• 青花唐僧取经纹钵式炉（明）
Blue-and-white Porcelain Bowl-style Burner with the Pattern of Monk Xuanzang's Pilgrimage (Ming Dynasty)

本、戏曲的基础上，经过艰苦的艺术再创造，才完成了这部伟大的文学巨著。

《西游记》全书共有一百回，前七回主要叙述唐僧的大徒弟孙悟空出世的故事，此后写孙悟空随唐僧西天取经，沿途除妖降魔，收服其他两个弟子，四个人共同历经磨难，最终求得真经的故事。书中唐僧、孙悟空、猪八戒、沙和尚等形象栩栩如生，故事规模宏大，结构完整，是中国古典小说中伟大的浪漫主义文学作品。

the early life and antecedents of the monkey Sun Wukong. Afterwards, he is depicted traveling alongside Xuanzang on his journey to the West to obtain the scriptures. On their way, two other disciples joined them, subduing countless demons and surmount numerous difficulties. Four of them obtained the real Buddhist sutras at last. The book portrays Xuanzang, Sun Wukong, Zhu Bajie and Sha Wujing vividly, with well-designed, grand composition.

> 西天路上取经人

唐僧、孙悟空、猪八戒和沙和尚师徒四人无疑是《西游记》中的主角。其中唐僧是西天取经队伍中的领导人物，在他锲而不舍的努力下，取经的任务才得以完成。

> Pilgrims on the Journey to the West

Monk Xuanzang (also referred to as Tang Sanzang and widely known as Tang Seng), Sun Wukong, Zhu Bajie and Sha Wujing (also known as Sha Seng) are undoubtedly the major characters, among whom Tang Seng is the leading character in *Journey to the West*. His perseverance led to the success of pilgrimage. In the novel, Xuanzang was the reincarnation of Golden Cicada, a disciple of Buddha. He showed a superb intelligence and earnestness that are beyond other monks. Designated by the emperor, he was sent on a mission to the West to bring a set of Buddhist scriptures back to China for the purpose of spreading Buddhism in his native land. Xuanzang was gentle in

- 皮影人物——唐僧（图片提供：全景正片）
Shadow Figure Monk Xuanzang

小说《西游记》里的唐僧是如来佛的二徒弟金蝉子转世，早年皈依佛门，由于悟性极高且又勤敏好学，不久便在寺庙僧人中脱颖而出，被皇帝选定前往西天取经。他性情和善，胸怀天下，惠及黎民百姓，为了求取真经克服艰难险阻，历经九九八十一难，终于功德圆满。与此同时，他还在所到之处宣扬佛法和亲民敬君的思想，展现了自己坚韧的品格和不凡的品质。

nature, and cared deeply for the people. He overcame numerous hardships and dangers in his quest for the scriptures. After enduring eighty-one trials of tribulations, he ultimately attained Buddhahood. Meanwhile, he spread Buddhist teachings and advocated for kindness wherever he went, showing his tenacity and extraordinary integrity.

　　Along the journey, Monk Xuanzang was constantly demanded by monsters and demons because of a legend which said that one would attain immortality by consuming his flesh because he was a reincarnation of a holy being. He was extremely naive, showing idealistic compassion to an extent that often lead him to predicaments. He was usually quick to fall for the facades of demons who had disguised themselves as innocent humans. One such popular instance was the story of the White Bone Demon disguised three times as human. It first transformed into a woman delivering food to get close to Xuanzang and his disciples. Sun Wukong saw through its disguise and "killed" her,

- 尸魔三戏唐三藏
  The Corpse Fiend Thrice Tricks Tang Sanzang (Monk Xuanzang)

由于唐僧是金蝉子转世，据说吃了他的肉便可以长生不老，于是在取经的路上便出现了许多想吃唐僧肉的妖怪。而唐僧本性善良，心慈手软，不忍杀生，于是便经常处于危险的境地。小说中的"三打白骨精"一节就是一个很好的例证。唐僧师徒西天取经路过白虎岭，被附近的白骨精发现。为了能够吃到唐僧肉，她先是变成了一个送饭的妇人，接近唐僧师徒，孙悟空将其识破，一棒打走，而蒙在鼓里的唐僧却责怪孙悟空不应该伤人。逃走后的白骨精并不死心，第二次又变成一个寻找女儿的老太婆，但依然被孙悟空打得落荒而逃。唐僧仍旧指责孙悟空不该连伤两人。最后，白骨精又变成一个老头，将唐僧捉走。这时唐僧才恍然大悟，幸好孙悟空及时出现才将其救出。

孙悟空是唐僧的大徒弟，是一个兼具神性与人性的猴子形象。他神通广大，有一双能识别妖怪的火眼，会七十二般变化，一个筋斗能翻十万八千里，还有一根可大可小的如意金箍棒。他英勇善战，是取经队伍中主要的战斗力量，一路上降妖伏魔，保护唐僧，最后取回真

but Xuanzang, unaware of the truth, blamed Sun Wukong for harming the innocent. The White Bone Demon then transformed into an old woman looking for her daughter, but it was once again driven away by Sun Wukong, who was again blamed by Xuanzang for he did not believe Su Wukong's words . Finally, the White Bone Demon turned into an old man looking for his wife and daughter, and captured Xuanzang. It was only then that Xuanzang realized the truth, and fortunately, Sun Wukong appeared in time to rescue him.

Sun Wukong is a monkey figure with embodying both divine and human qualities. As the first disciple of Xuanzang, Sun Wukong possessed an immense amount of strength, superbly fast, and was able to travel 108,000 li (54,000 kilometers) in one somersault. He knew 72 transformations, which allowed him to transform into various animals and objects, and had the ability to recognize evils in any form through his "fiery-eyes and golden-gaze". He had a golden-banded staff, Ruyi Jingu Bang, which could change its size. He is brave and skilled in fighting, an important protector of Xuanzang on their quest of obtaining the scriptures. After they successfully

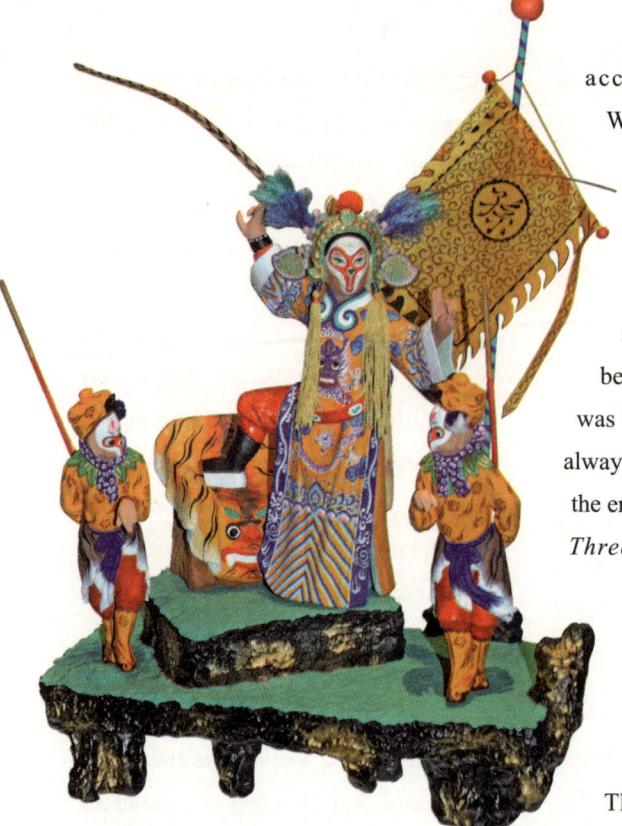

美猴王孙悟空泥塑
Clay Statue of Sun Wukong (Monkey King)

经，修成正果。

　　每每遇到妖怪，孙悟空总是第一个冲上前去打斗，而且有勇有谋，随机应变，总能置敌人于死地。"三借芭蕉扇"是经典的一例。唐僧师徒四人路经火焰山，熊熊烈焰阻挡了去路。这时必须借铁扇公主的芭蕉扇将山火扑灭才能度过去。于是孙悟空便到铁扇公主那

accomplished the mission, Sun Wukong was granted Buddhahood for his service, and safely returned to homeland with the scriptures.

Every time when demons showed up, Sun Wukong would be the first to fight against them. He was both courageous and resourceful, always able to adapt in battle and defeat the enemies. The story of *Sun Wukong's Three Attempts to Borrow Banana Leaves Fan* is a good example. According to the story, Monk Xuanzang and his disciples encountered an extremely hostile range of volcanic mountains. They could only pass if they use Princess Iron Fan's fan to subdue the flaming mountains. Her fan, made from banana leaves, was extremely large and had magical properties, as it could create giant whirlwinds. Sun Wukong went to borrow her fan, but she turned him down as the monkey fought with her son earlier. To get the fan, Sun Wukong transformed into a fly and flew into her mouth, went down her throat, and flew into her belly. Once inside, the monkey kicked and punched Princess Iron Fan until she was in so much pain that she

里借芭蕉扇。此前铁扇公主的儿子曾经被孙悟空打过，所以铁扇公主便怀恨在心，不肯将扇子借给他。为了顺利借到芭蕉扇，孙悟空变成一只飞虫，飞进了铁扇公主的肚子里，并一通折腾，使得铁扇公主不得不交出芭蕉扇。但是狡猾的铁扇公主并没有给他真的芭蕉扇而是给了他一把假扇子。孙悟空用这把扇子一扇，山火不但没有熄灭反而变得更大了。于是，孙悟空变作铁扇公主的丈夫又去借，终于借得真扇，才将大火扇灭顺利地度过了火焰山。该故事将他不屈不挠的精神和随机应变的智慧展露无遗。

gave him a fake fan which intensified the flames instead of putting them out. Having barely escaped from the fire, Sun Wukong returned, disguised himself as her husband through shape-shifting and finally obtained the fan.

Zhu Bajie is the second disciple of Xuanzang, and has the Buddhist name Wuneng. Zhu Bajie originally held the title of "Marshal Canopy", and was the commander-in-chief of 80,000 warriors. He was later banished, however, for misbehavior. Bajie was captivated by the beauty of the Goddess of the Moon. Following a drunken attempt to sexually harass her, he was banished to Earth. In any case, he was exiled from Heaven and sent to be reincarnated on Earth, where by mishap he fell into a pig well and was reborn as a man with a pig face. Although his fighting skills were not as great as Sun Wukong, he knew 36 transformations and could fly up to the cloudy regions. Using his nine-toothed rake, he was capable of fighting against most of the devils they encountered on their journey. Often seen

- 孙悟空三借芭蕉扇
  Sun Wukong's Three Attempts to Borrow Banana Leaves Fan

火焰山

火焰山地处吐鲁番盆地中部，东西长1000千米，南北宽10千米，平均海拔500米左右。火焰山山石主体呈赤褐色，山上无雪少雨，极端干旱，寸草不生。每当盛夏，在烈日照射下山体红光闪烁，就像烈焰熊熊，故名"火焰山"。相传《西游记》中的火焰山即指此处。

Flaming Mountains

The Flaming Mountains are 100 kilometers long from east to west, 10 kilometers wide from south to north, crossing the middle Turpan Depression. They are barren, eroded, red sandstone hills in Tianshan Mountain range, Xinjiang, China. The average height of the Flaming Mountains is 500 meters. Their striking gullies and trenches are caused by erosion of the red sandstone bedrock giving the mountains a flaming appearance at certain times of the day. It's said that it is the Flaming Mountain in *Journey to the West*.

- 新疆吐鲁番火焰山（图片提供：FOTOE）
The Flaming Mountains in Turpan Depression, Xinjiang Autonomous Region

猪八戒是唐僧的二徒弟，法号悟能。他原本是天上的天蓬元帅，后来因为调戏月宫中的嫦娥被逐出天庭，投胎到人间。不想投胎没投对，投成了猪胎，长了一副猪脸人身的模样。他手使一把九齿钉耙，as Sun Wukong's right-hand man, he also achieved notable merits in protecting Monk Xuanzang.

Zhu Bajie is a comical image possessing strength, honesty and is fearless in battling the demons. However,

- **泥塑《猪八戒背媳妇》**

  猪八戒背媳妇是在中国民间广为流传的一个故事，说的是猪八戒幻化成人形，入赘到高老庄一户人家做女婿。有一天，他由于喝醉酒显出了原形，吓坏众人。恰巧此时唐僧带领着孙悟空由此经过，于是孙悟空便变成他妻子的模样让猪八戒背着，并且在途中施展各种法术折磨他。最后八戒识破孙悟空的把戏，与孙悟空打斗。猪八戒被打败后，便跟着唐僧师徒一同前往西天取经。

  Clay Statue *Zhu Bajie Carrying His Spouse*
  A very popular folk story in China. Zhu Bajie's indulgence in women led him to the Gao Family Village, where he posed as a normal being and wedded a maiden. One day he got drunk and showed his original appearance, part human and part pig, which scared all villagers. Coincidentally, Monk Xuanzang and Sun Wukong passed by and learnt what happed there. Sun Wukong posed as his spouse and rode on his back to tease him. After seeing through Sun Wukong's trick, they combated with each other ending up with Zhu Bajie's defeat. Zhu Bajie consequently joined the pilgrimage to the West.

虽然法力不及孙悟空，但是也有三十六般变化，能腾云驾雾，是孙悟空的得力帮手，为保护唐僧去西天取经立下了汗马功劳。

在《西游记》中，猪八戒是最具生活化的一个人物形象。他性格温和，憨厚单纯，但好吃懒做，爱占小便宜，还贪图女色。在"四圣试禅心"一节中，黎山老母、观音菩萨、文殊菩萨和普贤菩萨为试探唐僧师徒的禅心，便化身为母女四人前来引诱唐僧师徒。其他人都不为所动，只有猪八戒禁不住诱惑。更为可笑的是，当三个女儿都

he was also often lazy, enjoying taking advantage of others, and was lustful. In a story of testing the meditative mind of the four pilgrims, Mother Lishan, Guanyin, Manjusri and Samantabhadra incarnated as a mother and three daughters respectively to seduce four pilgrims. Everyone resisted the temptation except Zhu Bajie. Ridiculously, Zhu Bajie even wanted to marry their mother after he was refused from three daughters.

Sha Seng is the third disciple of Xuanzang, and was given the Buddhist name Wujing. He was originally a general in Heaven, more specifically a "Curtain-

皮影人物——沙和尚（图片提供：全景正片）
Shadow Figure —Sha Seng

不要他时，他竟然提出想和丈母娘成亲。

沙和尚是唐僧的三徒弟，法号悟净。他原是天庭中的卷帘大将，后来因为失手打碎了琉璃盏被贬下凡间，在流沙河中兴风作浪，危害一方。经观音菩萨的点化，他拜唐僧为师，同孙悟空、猪八戒一同保护唐僧前往西天拜佛求经。沙僧虽然相貌丑陋，但正直无私，任劳任怨，恪守佛门戒律，是整个取经队伍中不可或缺的人物。

《西游记》中除了唐僧、孙悟空、猪八戒和沙和尚四人以外，还

Lifting General". He destroyed a valuable vase unintentionally, and was therefore exiled to earth. There, he lived in Quicksand River, terrorizing surrounding villages. Later, Guanyin, the Bodhisattva of compassion, converted him. He was instructed to wait for Xuanzang and join other disciples on Xuanzang's journey. His appearance looked more like a human, yet still ugly. During the journey to the West, Wujing was a kind-hearted and obedient character, and was very loyal to Xuanzang. As the third disciple, he was a great warrior who protected Xuanzang and an indispensable member of the group.

Beside Monk Xuanzang, Sun Wukong, Zhu Bajie, and Sha Seng, there is another important character that is often neglected—the White Loong Horse, Xuanzang's mount. He was the third son of the Loong King of the West Sea, who was sentenced to death for setting fire to his father's great pearl bestowed by Yudi. He was commissioned by Guanyin to accompany Xuanzang to the West. Throughout the story, he mainly appeared as the horse that Xuanzang rode on. Although playing a less conspicuous role in the story, he accompanied Xuanzang and his disciples all the way

- 唐僧师徒
  Monk Xuanzang and His Disciples

有一个容易被遗忘的角色，那便是唐僧的坐骑——白龙马。它原本是西海龙王的三儿子，因纵火烧毁玉帝赏赐的明珠而触犯天条，后来也是经过观音菩萨的点化，变身为白龙马驮着唐僧西天取经。白龙马一路上任劳任怨，历尽艰辛，功劳虽不及孙悟空和猪八戒那么大，但也是取经过程中必不可少的一员。

on their journey to the West, and bore responsibility without grudge despite hardships, making him an indispensable member of the team.

> 真幻一体　庄谐相融

《西游记》全书洋洋洒洒数十万言，从头到尾都是大胆离奇的幻想。小说中的主要人物除唐僧之外，不是神魔便是妖怪，大都有一些奇异的法术，有的还持有功能神奇的法宝。他们活动的区域是远离

> **Integrating Fantasy with Reality, Solemnity with Humor**

Journey to the West spans hundreds of thousands of words, filled with bold and fantastical imaginations. Fantastic fantasies can be tracked between the lines. All kinds of characters are capable of magic arts, and some of them even have supernatural weapons, with the

- 《西游记》人物彩画
  Colored Painting Figures from *Journey to the West*

玄奘像
Statue of Xuanzang

现实人间的天庭地府、仙山龙宫、荒岭魔窟，在那里上演了一幕幕变幻无穷、惊心骇目的故事，令读者心驰神迷，叹为观止。

在《西游记》中，作者吴承恩创造性地将各种神话故事和民间传说中的神魔、人物的关系进行了一次认真的梳理和整合，建构了一个

exception of Xuanzang. The appealing and fascinating scenes are set in the heaven, the hell, the loong palace, mountains and caves in barren lands that are far beyond man's world.

Journey to the West has a strong background in Chinese mythology and value systems. The author Wu Chen'en constructed a huge and complicated hierarchy among the pantheon and demons by putting their relationship in order. In this mythological world, Yudi living in the Hall of Miraculous Mist had the supreme sovereign of all. His subordinates included the leaders of civil servants Daode Tianzun, also known as Taishang Laojun, and Metal Lord of the West, also known as Taibai Jinxing; the leaders of military officers Li Jing and Erlang Shen. Below them were subordinated officers and heavenly army. In addition, Yudi also had jurisdiction over Loong Kings of the Four Seas, Ten Kings of Hell, numerous Mountain Deities and Earth Deities. Tathagata, known as the Buddha, reigned over other Bodhisattvas and Arhats in Western Heaven.

In addition to the pantheon, animals and plants who were seen in real life were posed as various demons that

• 如来佛祖像
Statue of Tathagata

庞大复杂而又尊卑有序的神魔体系。在这个神魔世界里，处于至高无上地位的是住在灵霄宝殿的玉皇大帝。他的部下，文臣以太白金星、道祖太上老君为首，武将以托塔李天王、二郎神杨戬为首，下面还有一众文武仙卿、天兵天将。此外，四海龙王、十殿阎王以及众多的山神土地也都受玉皇大帝管辖。如来佛祖率领众多菩萨、罗汉、金刚住在西天极乐世界。

《西游记》中除了天神之外还出现了各种各样的妖魔鬼怪，他们有的由现实生活中的动植物幻化而成，有的是从天上神佛处私自逃出来的，为祸一方。如狮子精变化成全真道士害死乌鸡国国王，篡权夺位；黄狮精从玉华国盗走孙悟空、猪八戒、沙和尚三人的兵器

caused troubles on man's world. For example, there is a story of the lion demon posed as a Taoist priest to kill the king of the Wuji Kingdom and usurped the royal power; in another story, three pilgrims' weapons were stolen by a

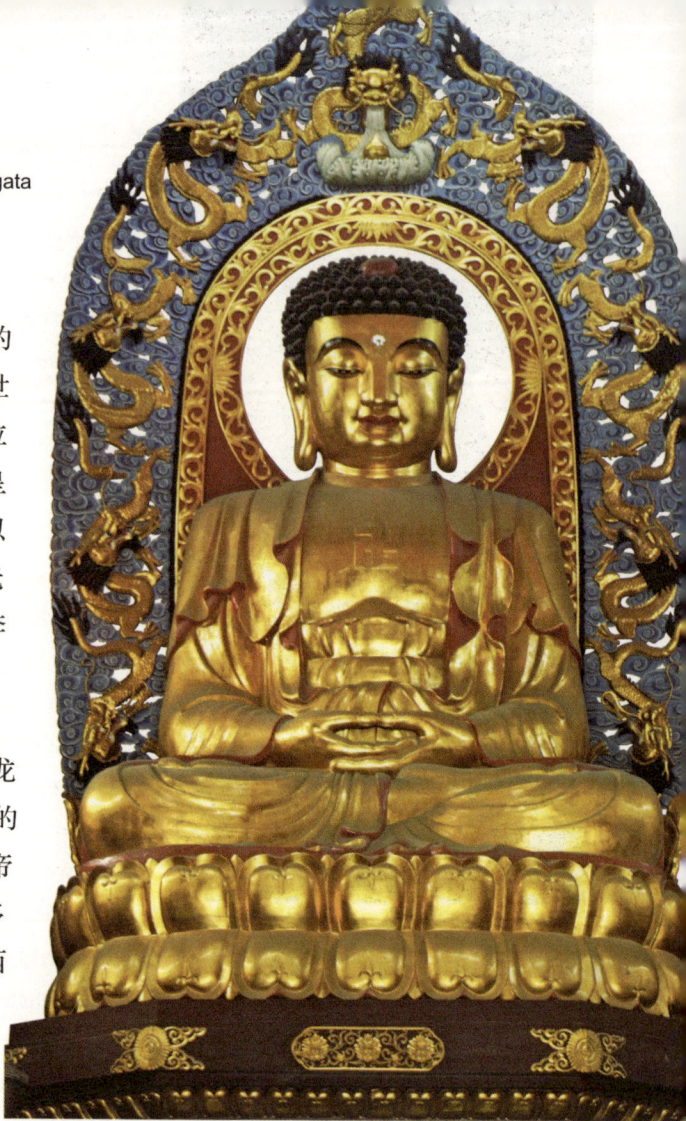

等。这些妖怪的设置，无非是要制造取经路上的"九九八十一难"，而《西游记》最终的结局也是在经历"九九八十一难"之后，唐僧师徒四人终于到达西天取得真经。小说的主题也在不断的降妖除魔中彰显出来。

《西游记》的成就不仅在于它凭借天马行空的想象创造了一个光怪陆离的幻想境界，更重要的是这些想象深深地扎根于现实的土壤之中，作者在创作中融入了自己对现实生活清醒而深刻的认识。比如小说中的车迟国国王宠信道士，拜虎力、鹿力、羊力三个妖魔为国师，终日祈求圣水、仙丹以图长生延寿，国家大事也听凭三个妖道摆布，还派人四处捉拿和尚去服苦役。

又比如比丘国国王好色纵欲，导致身体衰弱，命在须臾。白鹿化成的老道向他进献延寿之方，要用一千一百一十一个小儿

yellow lion demon. The purpose of these monsters' creation was to have "eighty-one tribulations" on Xuanzang's journey to obtain the scriptures. After overcoming these challenges, Xuanzang and his three disciples finally reached the West, and attained Buddhahood. The theme of the novel was revealed in the process of vanquishing demons and monsters.

Journey to the West is rich in imaginations and creates a bizarre fancy world. More importantly, these

- 孙悟空师兄弟大战群妖（图片提供：FOTOE）
Sun Wukong and Other Pilgrims Fighting Against Demons

的心肝做药引,这位昏君竟然深信不疑,将众多孩童抓来关在鹅笼里。诸如此类的描写都被认为是借题发挥,影射当时的现实。据明代沈德符《万历野获编》记载,明世宗就曾选四百六十名女子作炼丹之用。由此可见,《西游记》中的奇幻故事并非为作者

imaginations are root in reality, and show that the author has profound insights into the real life. The tale about the kingdom of Chechi is a close analogy. The king favored Taoist priests, and was apprenticed to three demons. He spent his days praying for holy water and elixirs in hopes of attaining immortality, and allowed the three demon priests to manipulate state affairs. Furthermore, he even sent people to capture monks for forced labor.

Another example is the story of the king of Biqiu Kingdom, who lived a dissolute life, which made him very sick. To have good health and a long life, he even followed the instruction from a white deer demon who posed as a Taoist priest. The white deer demon proposed a longevity plan to him, which required the hearts of 1,111 children as the main ingredient. The king

• 观音像
Portrait of Guanyin

- 西游记版画
Prints of *Journey to the West*

believed him without doubt, and had many children captured and imprisoned in cages. In reality, according to *Wanli Yehuo Bian* written by Shen Defu of the Ming Dynasty, four hundred and sixty maids were sacrificed to the alchemy during the reign of the Emperor Shizong of the Ming Dynasty. Therefore, stories in the novel were not fabricated but reflected reality.

All the characters depicted in *Journey to the West* were humanized. They were similar to human beings in characters. Taking Sun Wukong as an example, positive sides of his character as bravery, resourcefulness, pursuit of freedom, perseverance and optimism are in balance with negative sides of his character such as vanity and impatience. The flaws in his personality made him a more approachable character to the readers.

Journey to the West is featured by its recreational nature, and it is rich in humor and farcicality. However, these

胡乱编造，而是现实社会生活的投影。

此外，《西游记》的作者在塑造神魔形象时，有意识地将其"人化"，将他们视为凡人来书写，着力表现他们与凡人相类似的性格特征。例如孙悟空这一形象，小说既反复突出他神通广大、机智勇敢、自由洒脱、顽强乐观的优秀品质，又竭力表现他身上存在的缺点，比如好名、急躁、喜欢炫耀自己等，

唐僧师徒雕像（图片提供：FOTOE）
Statues of Xuanzang and His Disciples

这就使读者感到可亲可信。

《西游记》是一部富含鲜明的娱乐化特征的小说，全书基本上以游戏笔墨写成，这样就形成了幽默、谐谑的风格。但是《西游记》中的游戏笔墨不是为游戏而游戏，也不是些浅薄无聊的世俗调笑，而是一种富有社会意义的批判手段，一种表达作者是非爱憎的特殊方式，其中熔铸着作者的人生感受和愤世嫉俗之情。因而这些谐谑的游戏笔墨大都滑稽而不油滑，诙谐而

expressions are not in the slightest vulgar jokes. They serve as a way to criticize the reality and express likes and dislikes explicitly. Social criticalness and personal experiences are given full play in the novel. The meaningful language tends to be witty and humorous rather than vulgar.

In *Journey to the West*, the portrayal of fierce fighting scenes were often tinged with a joking tone. As depicted in chapter 34, Zhu Bajie, Sha Seng and Xuanzang were caught by two demons, Golden Horned King and Silver Horned King, that they encountered on their

● 皮影《西游记》人物
Shadow Figures from *Journey to the West*

- **京剧《大闹天宫》中的孙悟空**

京剧《大闹天宫》讲述的是：孙悟空被玉帝封为齐天大圣，负责看管王母娘娘的蟠桃园。恰逢王母娘娘生日，各路神仙都被邀请去参加王母娘娘的生日宴会，唯独没有邀请孙悟空。这令他很是生气，一气之下便大闹蟠桃宴，还偷吃了太上老君的金丹。玉帝知道此事之后，便令天兵天将来捉拿他，于是双方展开了一场激战，最后孙悟空大胜而归。

A Scene from Peking Opera *Havoc in Heaven*

Peking Opera *Havoc in Heaven* is based on a classic story in *Journey to the West*. After Yudi had to accept the Monkey King's claimed title of "Great Sage", Sun Wukong agreed to become the guardian of the Heavenly Garden. One day a procession of fairies came to collect peaches for an important Imperial banquet where they were questioned by Sun Wukong about the banquet's guests. When he learnt that all but him had been invited, he went furious. He caused trouble at the banqnet and left for the Flower and Fruit Mountain but got lost, by mistake entering Taishang Laojun's workshop where he ate his pills of immortality. The irritated emperor dispatched the Heavenly army to punish Wukong; however, the fierce fighting ended with the Heavenly army's defeat.

不庸俗，戏谑而不轻浮，具有深刻的思想内涵。

作者常常在降伏妖魔的殊死搏斗中将轻松调笑的游戏笔墨穿插其间。如小说第三十四回，猪八戒、沙和尚、唐僧三人被平顶山妖魔金角大王和银角大王捉了去，孙悟空变成魔王的母亲前往解救。魔王

journey. Sun Wukong posed as demons' mother to rescne them. The demons said that eating Xuanzang's flesh at their mother's birthday banquet would promote longevity, to which Sun Wukong replied, "I don't want to have Xuanzang's flesh. It is said that Bajie's pig ears are tasty. Cut them up and make a dish for me." Bajie shouted, "You demon! You come here to

说要把唐僧肉蒸给母亲吃了延寿，孙悟空便说："我儿，唐僧的肉我倒不吃，听见有个猪八戒的耳朵甚好，可割下来整治整治我下酒。"八戒一听急了，连忙喊道："遭瘟

cut up my ears. It's bad for me to shout it out!" Bajie's response exposed the true identity of demons' mother, and suddenly two demons pulled out swords toward Wukong. This spirit of humor and jest,

- 《西游记》绣像
  Tapestry Portrait of *Journey to the West*

的！你来为割我耳朵的？我喊出来不好听啊！"只因猪八戒这一通话，泄露了孙悟空变妖母的真相。两位魔王顿时拔出宝剑朝孙悟空劈面砍去，孙悟空只得逃出洞外。这种在险象迭生的恶战中还不忘戏谑的精神，增加了小说滑稽调笑的气氛，既显示了孙悟空藐视强敌的乐观主义精神，又化解了叙事中的紧张气氛，使读者绷紧的心弦顿时松弛下来。

又如小说四十六回写到，唐僧师徒四人来到车迟国，受到了车迟国国师虎力、鹿力、羊力大仙的刁难。经过一番斗法之后，羊力大仙决定要和孙悟空比试下油锅。当油锅被烧得滚开之后，孙悟空毫不犹豫地跳了进去，而且还耍了个花招，"打个水花，淬在油锅底上，变作个枣核钉儿，再也不起来了"。车迟国王以为悟空已经死了，便把唐僧师徒捆绑了起来。猪八戒见此情景忍不住咒骂起来："闯祸的泼猴子，无知的弼马温！该死的泼猴子，油烹的弼马温！猴儿了账，马温断根！"这一骂，使得孙悟空忍不住又在油锅中现了本

even amidst narrow escape in a fierce battle, enhances the novel's whimsical atmosphere. Wukong's unfailing optimism has found full expression in these stories. These funny dialogues helped to alleviate the tense atmosphere and made readers feel relaxed.

As described in chapter 46, when Xuanzang and his disciples arrived at the Kingdom of Chechi, three demons—the Immortal of Tiger Power, Immortal of Elk Power, and Immortal of Antelope Power—deliberately put obstacles in their way. After rounds of combat with Sun Wukong, the Immortal of Antelope Power challenged Sun Wukong to jump into a pot of boiling oil. Wukong did so without hesitation. He even played a trick, as described in the novel, by making a splash as he jumped in, and transformed into a jujube pit, disappearing from sight. The king of Chechi Kingdom, thinking that Sun Wukong was dead, had Xuanzang and his other two disciples tied up. Bajie was unable to restrain his desperate anger and broke out into curses. Hearing this, Sun Wukong revealed himself in the boiling oil pot, instantly easing the tense atmosphere. It is precisely these playful

089

《西游记》

Journey to the West

《西游记》绣像
The Tapestry Portrait of *Journey to the West*

相，枯燥的场景立刻变得轻松起来。正是有了这些游戏笔墨的描写，才使得作家毫无拘束地任意抒写奇思异想，表现出一种灵气飞动、活泼跳荡的叙事风格。

and whimsical narratives that allow the author to freely indulge in imaginative writing, showcasing a lively and dynamic narrative style.

《红楼梦》
A Dream of Red Mansions

《红楼梦》是一部具有高度思想性和艺术性的伟大作品，代表了中国古典小说艺术的最高成就。全书以贾宝玉、林黛玉两人的爱情悲剧为线索，描绘了大观园中众儿女的悲惨命运，并通过对社会现实生活及世俗人情的展现，反映了一个封建大家族逐步衰亡的过程。

A Dream of Red Mansions is considered to be a masterpiece of Chinese literature and is generally acknowledged to be the pinnacle of Chinese fiction. The thread running through the novel is the tragic love story of Baoyu and Daiyu. The tragic fate of the people living in Red Mansions is closely interrelated to the decadent trend of the feudal clans. The novel is remarkable for its precise and detailed observation of the life and social structures of ancient Chinese aristocracy.

> 《红楼梦》概述

　　《红楼梦》别名《石头记》。与前三部小说不同，这部小说属于作者独立创作的作品。《红楼梦》的作者曹雪芹出身名门望族，他

> Synopsis of *A Dream of Red Mansions*

The novel is also often known as *The Story of the Stone*. Unlike the other three classical novels of Chinese literature, the novel was not compiled over preexisted historical records but written

- 北京大观园缀锦阁
Zhuijin Pavilion in Beijing Grand View Garden

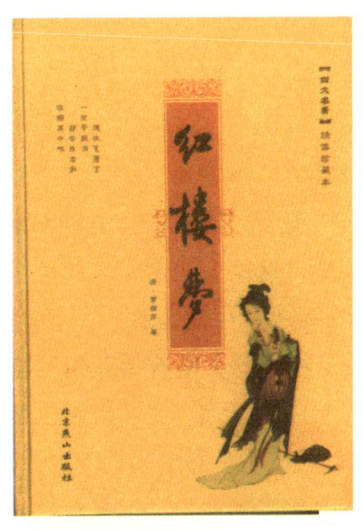

• 《红楼梦》书影

Photography of A *Dream of Red Mansions*

• 曹雪芹蜡像

曹雪芹（约1715—约1763），清代小说家。他的祖父工诗词、善书法，他自幼受其祖父的影响，具有多方面的艺术才能。长篇小说《红楼梦》是他呕心沥血、"披阅十载，增删五次"而写下的不朽巨著。

Wax Figure of Cao Xueqin

Cao Xueqin (approx.1715-approx.1763)was a Qing-dynasty writer. Cao Xueqin at an early age was influenced by his grandfather who was one of the era's most prominent men of letters. Cao achieved posthumous fame through his life's work. He pored over the book for ten years and rewrote it five times, written in "blood and tears".

的家庭在清代康熙时期颇受皇帝恩宠。他的曾祖母是康熙皇帝的乳母，祖父做过清代康熙皇帝的"侍读"。但后来在宫廷内部的争斗中

independently by Cao Xueqin. He was born in a distinguished family. During Kangxi Emperor's reign (1662-1722), his family's prestige and power reached its height. Cao's grandfather was a childhood playmate to Emperor Kangxi, while Cao's grand-grand mother was Kangxi's wet nurse. However, in the subsequent internal court struggles, the Cao family suffered a defeat and became impoverished. Cao Xueqin, still a young child then, lived in poverty with his family. Having witnessed and experienced family calamities, Cao Xueqin had deeper understanding about the feudal society. His misfortunes laid

曹家失利，迅速败落下来。从此，曹雪芹由一个锦衣玉食的世家公子逐渐变成了一个落魄的文人。由于亲身经历了由盛到衰的家庭变故，他对于整个封建制度有了更为深入的了解，这也为他创作《红楼梦》奠定了坚实的生活基础。

《红楼梦》是曹雪芹用尽毕生心血写成的巨著。他"批阅十载，增删五次"，由于当时生活的困顿，曹雪芹经常是"举家食粥酒常

a solid foundation for the creation of his masterpiece; hence, *A Dream of Red Mansions* is believed to be semi-autobiographical, mirroring the rise and decay of Cao Xueqin's own family and, by extension, of the Qing Dynasty.

Cao Xueqin devoted his life to this masterpiece. He and his family lived an impoverished life. They had porridge all day long and had to buy wine on credit. His youngest son passed away due to illness amidst poverty, and Cao Xueqin soon passed away in the pain of the death

- 《红楼梦》影视拍摄地
Film Shooting Location for *A Dream of Red Mansions*

赊",他的小儿子就是在这样的情况下病逝的。而曹雪芹本人由于经受不住丧子之痛,不久之后也离开了人世,留下了一部仅有八十回的遗著。后来程伟元、高鹗在其前八十回的基础上补叙了四十回,最终使《红楼梦》完整地呈现在世人面前。

《红楼梦》描写了一个大家庭由盛到衰的过程。小说中的贾府是一个关系庞杂的大家庭,府上的祖辈曾经为国家立下过汗马功劳,也得到了皇帝的嘉奖。但是贾家的后辈却不思进取,过着荒淫无度的日子,导致了这个大家庭的败落。小说的精妙之处在于借书中主人公贾宝玉和林黛玉的爱情悲剧来展现贾府颓败与溃散的过程,令人耳目一新。

《红楼梦》以其丰富的内容、曲折的情节、深刻的思想、精湛的技艺,成为中国古典小说最具成就的巅峰之作,以至于以一部作品构成了一门独立的研究学科——"红学",这在世界文学史上是绝无仅有的。

of his child, leaving an uncompleted work of 80 chapters. Cheng Weiyuan and Gao E later added 40 additional chapters to complete the novel.

The novel featured a huge cast of characters, and each of them experienced the rise and decay of the wealthy and aristocratic Jia clan. The ancestors of Jia clan were made Dukes and given imperial titles. However, the clan's descendants were excessively indulgent, and his dissipation led to the fall of the wealthy clan. As the main thread of the novel, the love story of Jia Baoyu and Lin Daiyu—a love story told so touchingly that almost all readers shed sympathetic tears at the tragic ending of the story—was designed to be closely related and interwoven with the rise and fall of the feudal family.

With its rich content, intricate plots, deep insights and exquisite writing skills, *A Dream of Red Mansions* has become the most accomplished masterpiece in Chinese classical literature. The novel has profound social significance and great historical value; so much so that "Redology" has become a well-studied academic field that is explicitly devoted to this novel, an unparalleled phenomenon in the history of world literature.

> 红楼众儿女

《红楼梦》众多人物中，最为人瞩目的无疑是以林黛玉和薛宝钗为首的"金陵十二钗"：林黛玉、薛宝钗、贾元春、贾探春、史湘云、妙玉、贾迎春、贾惜春、王熙凤、贾巧姐、李纨、秦可卿。她们不但有着出众的容貌，更有着鲜明的个性。

林黛玉是"金陵十二钗"之冠。小说中的林黛玉被作者描绘成一位清丽脱俗、雅若天仙的女子形象。前世她是一株绛珠仙草，受神瑛侍者的甘露之惠。今世她是林如海与贾敏的独生女，贾母的外孙女。少年时，因其母亲贾敏身患重病亡故，外祖母怜其孤独，便将其接来贾府抚养，后又因其父亲林如

> Characters in *A Dream of Red Mansions*

Among an extraordinarily large number of characters in *A Dream of Red Mansions*, the most notable are undoubtedly the "Twelve Beauties of Jinling", led by Lin Daiyu and Xue Baochai. Other Beauties of Jinling are Jia Yuanchun, Jia Tanchun, Shi Xiangyun, Miao Yu, Jia Yingchun, Jia Xichun, Wang Xifeng, Jia Qiaojie, Li Wan and Qin Keqing. They not only have exceptional beauty but also distinct and rich personalities.

The novel designated Lin Daiyu as the top of the Twelve Beauties of Jinling and portrayed her as a lonely, sentimental, proud, talented, unsophisticated and ultimately tragic figure. She was sickly, but beautiful in a way that was unconventional— a godlike beauty. According to the novel, she was

• 《红楼梦》中的众儿女
Characters of *A Dream of Red Mansions*

海也病故，黛玉便一直居住在贾府。虽然是寄人篱下的孤儿，但她生性孤傲，多愁善感，心思敏感，才华横溢，有时说话不免刻薄，但个性纯真，为人率直。她和贾宝玉有着共同的理想和志趣，他们真心相爱，但这一段爱情最终还是因悲剧性的家族命运而遭到扼杀。

the reincarnation of a flower which was watered by Divine Attendant-in-Waiting in her previous incarnation. She was the daughter of Lin Ruhai and Jia Min and the granddaughter of Grandmother Jia in this life. In her youth, after her mother passed away from a severe illness, her grandmother, feeling sorry for her loneliness, brought her to the Jia family

•《黛玉葬花》费丹旭（清）
《黛玉葬花》是《红楼梦》中的一节。故事情节是：暮春时节，黛玉看到花瓣落在地上被人践踏，心中不忍，便在墙角处设了一个花冢来埋葬这些花瓣。

A Painting, Depicting the Scene of *Daiyu Burying Fallen Flower Petals*, by Fei Danxu (Qing Dynasty)

Daiyu Burying Fallen Flower Petals is a chapter of *A Dream of Red Mansions*. In late spring, seeing people treading on the fallen petals, heartbroken Daiyu buried them on the corner.

薛宝钗也是"金陵十二钗"中的重要人物之一。她出身商人家庭，拥有百万家财。她的母亲薛姨妈与贾宝玉的母亲王夫人是亲姐妹。她来到贾府原是为了待选入宫，后来因为落选便长期住在了贾

to raise her. Soon after, her father passed away too, and Lin Daiyu continued to live with the Jia family. Daiyu and Baoyu loved each other and shared common interests; however, their love was doomed to be a tragedy due to the backdrop of the family's declining fortunes.

府。薛宝钗容貌美丽，举止娴雅，待人处事极为妥帖，因而得到贾府上上下下的喜爱。对于小说中的男主人公贾宝玉，她也存有爱慕之情，并且时常同他谈论仕途经济，希望他走上一条仕宦之路，但是贾宝玉对这些并不感兴趣。小说最后，她虽与贾宝玉结为夫妻，但他们的婚姻终以悲剧收场。

除黛钗外，"金陵十二钗"中另一个重要的人物便是王熙凤。王熙凤是贾宝玉的堂哥贾琏之妻，王夫人的内侄女。她精明强干，深得贾母和王夫人的信任，是荣国府实际的大管家。她泼辣张狂，口齿伶俐，善于阿谀奉承，喜欢使权弄势，炫耀特权。她极尽权术机变、残忍阴毒之能事，贾府上下莫不怕她三分。她公然宣称："我从来不信什么阴司地狱报应的，凭什么事，我说行就行！"她极度贪婪，除了索取贿赂外，还靠着放高利贷获取不义之财。她的所作所为，无疑加速了贾家的败落，最后她自己也只落得个"机关算尽太聪明，反误了卿卿性命"的下场。

"金陵十二钗"中其他重要的人物还有贾宝玉的姐姐，贾政与王

● 薛宝钗像
Portrait of Xue Baochai

Born in a wealthy merchant family, Jia Baochai is another principal character among the Twelve Beauties of Jinling. Her mother Aunt Xue was a sister to Jia Baoyu's mother, Lady Wang. Baochai stayed in Jia's Mansion for a chance to be elected by the imperial palace, but she failed and has lived in Jia's Mansion since then. She was not only beautiful, but also a person of tactfulness and

• 王熙凤像
Portrait of Wang Xifeng

夫人之长女贾元春。她自幼由贾母教养。作为长姐，她在宝玉三四岁时就已教他读书识字，虽为姐弟，有如母子。贾元春后因贤孝才德，选入宫作女吏，不久封凤藻宫尚书，加封贤德妃，成为贾府在朝中的"依靠"。元春虽给贾家带来了"烈火烹油，鲜花着锦之盛"，但她却被幽闭在皇家深宫内，最后暴病而亡。

thoughtfulness, thefore welcomed by most of people in Jia's Mansion. She had the affection towards Jia Baoyu and often encouraged him to secure an official position in the court, but Baoyu had the least interest in it. At the end of the story, she was married to Jia Baoyu, but their marriage was seen as predestined tragedy.

Another important character of the Jingling Twelve Beauties was Wang Xifeng, Baoyu's elder cousin-in-law, young wife to Jia Lian (who was Baoyu's paternal first cousin), and niece to Lady Wang. Xifeng was hence related to Baoyu both by blood and marriage. She was capable, clever, but also vicious and cruel. She publically claimed that she didn't believe in hell, to say nothing of karma. Xifeng was in charge of the daily running of the Rongguo household and wielded remarkable financial as well as political power within the family, ruling the entire household with an iron fist. On the other hand, she was extremely greedy, not only accepting bribes but also making illicit gains through usurious lending, which expedited the decline of Jia clan, the Rongguo Mansion. Eventually, she was ruined by her own "wisdom".

Jia Yuanchun was also one of the Jingling Twelve Beauties and the eldest

- 北京曹雪芹纪念馆内的贾元春蜡像
Waxen Image of Jia Yuanchun in Cao Xueqin Memorial Museum, Beijing

- 北京曹雪芹纪念馆内的贾探春放风筝蜡像
Waxen Image in Cao Xueqin Memorial Museum, Beijing, Depicting Jia Tanchun Flying a Kite

此外，"金陵十二钗"中的贾探春也是一个性格鲜明的人物。探春为贾政与小老婆赵姨娘所生，排行为贾府三小姐。她精明能干，有心机，能决断，连王夫人与凤姐都让她几分。面对着贾府日渐衰微的境况，她也曾经试图挽救，但终究无济于事，最后被迫远嫁他乡。

《红楼梦》的作者除了塑造了

daughter of Jia Zheng and Lady Wang. She was raised by Grandmother Jia from an early age. As Baoyu's eldest sister, she started to teach him reading and writing at the age of three or four years old. Originally selected as one of the ladies-in-waiting in the imperial palace, Yuanchun later became an Imperial Consort, having impressed the Emperor with her virtue and wisdom. Her illustrious position in the court marked the height of Jia

一系列女性形象之外，还重点刻画了贾宝玉这一男性形象。贾宝玉是贾府的嫡派子孙，他出生时口含一块美玉，故而名为"宝玉"。他生得"面若中秋之月，色如春晓之花"，从小在女儿堆里长大，喜欢亲近女孩儿，说"女儿都是水做的骨肉，男人都是泥做的骨肉"。作为贾氏家族被寄予厚望的继承人，他本应该走一条仕途经济之路，但

• 贾宝玉像
Portrait of Jia Baoyu

family's power. Despite her prestigious status, Yuanchun felt imprisoned within the walls of the imperial palace. Later, she died from a sudden illness.

As one of Jinling Twelve Beauties, Jia Tanchun had her own personality. She was Baoyu's younger half-sister, danghter of Jia Zheng and Concubine Zhao. She was shrewd, capable, decisive and outspoken, even earning the respect of Lady Wang and Wang Xifeng. She attempted to revive the Jia clan, but eventually failed to prevent the situation from deteriorating and was eventually forced into a marriage in a distant place.

Besides the female characters, Jia Baoyu was considered to be one of the major characters portrayed in the novel. As the son of Jia Zheng and his wife, Lady Wang, and born with a piece of luminescent jade in his mouth, hence his name, Baoyu was the heir apparent to the Jia family. Being a sensitive and compassionate individual, he had special relationships with many of the women in the mansion. As he said, "Girls are made of water, men of mud. I feel clean and refreshed when I am with girls but find men dirty and stinking." Baoyu was highly intelligent, but disliked the fawning bureaucrats and being

- 泥塑《二玉寻梅》
作品呈现的是贾宝玉与栊翠庵的尼姑妙玉在雪天寻找梅花的故事。
Clay Sculptures *Baoyu and Miaoyu Looking for Plum Blossom*
This work depicts the scene of Baoyu and Miaoyu looking for plum blossom in the snow. Miaoyu is a Buddhist nun who shelters herself under the nunnery in Prospect Garden.

是他却对此十分反感。此外，贾宝玉与林黛玉的爱情更是世间少有的纯洁之爱。他爱林黛玉，因为林黛玉的身世处境和内心品格包蕴了世间一切感人的真情。这种爱情追求恰恰体现了他对个性自由的向往。这个以叛逆思想为内核的爱情，也必然会遭到封建势力的严酷压迫。

the successor of Jia clan as his family expected. He fought for the freedom to love Lin Daiyu. However, his opposition to the feudal ethics was doomed to be repressed. In the end, he was forced to marry Baochai. It was on the wedding day that Daiyu died of haematemesis.

In addition to the characters mentioned above, there were other impressive

• 《红楼梦》人物瓷盘
Porcelain Plates Portraying Characters in *A Dream of Red Mansions*

王熙凤
Wang Xifeng

贾元春
Jia Yuanchun

史湘云
Shi Xiangyun

贾探春
Jia Tanchun

贾惜春
Jia Xichun

105

《红楼梦》

A Dream of Red Mansions

小说最后，贾宝玉被迫与薛宝钗成婚，而在他们成婚的当天，林黛玉吐血而亡。

除了以上提及的主要人物，《红楼梦》中的次要人物也给人留下了深刻的印象。比如活泼的史湘云、木讷的贾迎春，甚至包括贾府的丫鬟，诸如温婉的袭人、泼辣的晴雯等，都是性格极为鲜明的人物，她们共同缔造了《红楼梦》色彩斑斓的大观园世界。

• 《红楼梦》故事纹瓷盘
A Porcelain Plate Depicting a Scene from *A Dream of Red Mansions*

characters in the novel, such as the openhearted Shi Xiangyun and the apathetic Jia Yingchun. Some maids and servants were also vividly depicted, such as the shrewish Qingwen and the sweet-tempered Xiren.

> 虚幻与现实

《红楼梦》虽然是一部现实主义力作，但是其中一些虚幻的神话故事和梦境的描写，使得这部作品更添了几分神秘的梦幻色彩。

小说开篇借"一块顽石"的故事讲述了红楼的源起。女娲炼石补天时，曾经在大荒山无稽崖下炼石，当时她一共炼了三万六千五百零一块，但是补天只用了三万六千五百块，剩下的一块便被弃在青埂峰下。这块顽石由于没有被用来补天，便产生哀怨伤悲之情。后来一僧一道从此经过，将

- 江苏南京红楼艺文苑内的通灵宝玉石
The Stone of Precious Jade of Tongling in Red Mansions Literature and Art Garden

> Illusion and Reality

Despite *A Dream of Red Mansions* has been hailed as one of the realism masterpiece, the inclusion of some fantastical mythological stories and

女娲炼石补天

女娲炼石补天是中国的一个民间神话传说。传说在上古时候,有一位叫共工的神对颛顼帝的统治不满,便与他争斗了起来。后来共工因为没能战胜颛顼,十分恼怒,便一头撞在了不周山上。不周山原本是支撑天地间的柱子,被他这样一撞,便撞断了。不周山倒了之后,天便塌了下来,地也随之裂开了缝隙,生活在地上的人面临着灭绝的危险。这时候女娲出现了,她采来五色石,用天火熬成膏把天上的洞补好了。随后,她又潜入海底,砍下大海中神龟的四只脚,立在四方当柱子,把天地分开。这样一来,天地又恢复了正常,人们又过上了安稳的生活。

Goddess Nüwa Melting down Rocks to Repair the Wall of Sky

The Goddess Nüwa Melting down Rocks to Repair the Wall of Sky is a Chinese folk tale. As an ancient mythology goes, there was a god Gonggong who was resentful at the ruling of Zhuanxu. They decided to settle it with a fight. When Gonggong saw that he was losing, he smashed his head against Mount Buzhou, a pillar holding up the sky. It caused the collapse of the sky and great calamities on the ground. Nüwa cut off the legs of a giant tortoise and used them to supplant the fallen pillar, alleviating the situation and sealing the broken sky using stones of seven different colors. The heaven and earth went back to normal and people led a comfortable life since then.

- 女娲炼石补天
  Goddess Nüwa Melting down Rocks to Repair the Wall of Sky

• 江苏南京红楼艺文苑牌坊——太虚幻境

Illusory Land of Great Void from the Novel, the Archway in Red Mansions Literature and Art Garden, Nanjing, Jiangsu Province

其幻化为通灵宝玉携带至人间游历一番，在历尽人世间的悲欢炎凉后，又返回到青埂峰下。作者通过这个由混沌开始又结束于虚无的故事，使整部作品带有虚幻色彩。

《红楼梦》的虚幻色彩与作者多次提到的梦境密不可分。例如小说第五回写贾宝玉梦游太虚幻境，将一个虚无缥缈的世界展现在了

dreamy elements adds a touch of mysterious, dreamlike quality to the novel. A tint of mystery is constructed in a way that reality and illusion are often hinted side by side and difficult to differentiate.

The opening chapter of the novel started from the story of the stone. When the goddess Nü Wa melted down rocks to repair the sky, at Baseless Cliff in the Great Waste Mountain she made thirty-

- 《大观园图》佚名（清）

全画长1370毫米，横3620毫米。画作以蘅芜苑、凹晶馆、蓼风轩、牡丹亭、凸碧山庄五处建筑为中心，描绘各种人物活动其间的景象。

Picture of Grand View Garden, by Anon (Qing Dynasty)
This painting with 1370 millimeters in length and 3620 millimeters in width depicts people's activities in the five major constructions of Grand View Garden.

读者面前。书中写道，有一天，贾宝玉在梦中被警幻仙姑引领着来到了一个名为太虚幻境的地方。在这里，他首先看到的是太虚幻境的石牌楼，在石牌楼的两边有一副对

six thousand five hundred and one blocks of stone. She used only thirty-six thousand five hundred of these and threw the remaining block down at the foot of Blue Ridge Peak. This block of stone, after tempering, had acquired spiritual

联：假作真时真亦假，无为有处有还无。再往里面走是一处处的宫殿，上面分别写着宫殿的名称。贾宝玉在其中一处名为"薄命司"的宫殿里看到了关于金陵十二钗人生命运的诗文。作者通过写贾宝玉梦游太虚幻境，营造了一种虚幻的氛围，并在小说的开端暗示出大观园

understanding. Because all its fellow blocks had been chosen to mend the sky and it alone rejected, it lamented day and night in distress and shame. One day when a Buddhist monk and Taoist priest saw the pure translucent stone, they took it to the man's world. After experiencing the fickleness of the world and feelings of happiness and sorrow, the stone returned

江苏南京红楼艺文苑内的警幻仙子像
Statue of Goddess of Disenchantment in Literature and Art Garden of Red Mansions, Nanjing, Jiangsu Province

中众女子的命运，构思巧妙。

此外，作者还为故事中的青年男女设置了一个世外桃源般的生活场景——大观园。大观园原名"省亲别院"，是贾元春入宫后为了报答贾家的养育之恩，经皇上恩准，在荣国府附近建造的一座园林式别墅。元妃省亲回宫之后，由于担心没人居住会使园子荒废，便让贾府的一

to Blue Ridge Peak. The whole story was shrouded in mystery.

The recurring portrayal of dreams made illusion an inseparable element of the novel. The chapter 5, for example, referred to a dream where Baoyu wandered in the Illusory Land of Great Void following the Goddess of Disenchantment. An illusionary world unfolded before readers. In his dream, Baoyu passed through a large stone archway on which was inscribed: Illusory Land of Great Void. A couplet on the two pillars read: When false is taken for true, true becomes false; If non-being turns into being, being comes non-being. Baoyu saw the verses in another palace, ingeniously conceived, implying the fate of the Twelve Beauties of Jinling. Through the depiction of Jia Baoyu's dream journey, the author created an illusionary atmosphere and foreshadowed the fates of many characters in this opening chapter.

In addition, the author created a utopia-like setting called the Grand View Garden for the young men and women in the story. The Grand View Garden is a garden villa built within the Rongguo Mansion with the emperor's approval, as a gesture of gratitude from Jia Yuanchun to the Jia family for raising

- **北京大观园内的潇湘馆**

  林黛玉居住的潇湘馆周围有百竿翠竹遮映，竹子的高洁与黛玉的孤傲相契合，"潇湘"二字极易让人联想到湘妃娥皇、女英泪洒翠竹成斑的故事，同时也符合黛玉爱哭的个性。

  ### Xiaoxiang Courtyard in Grand View Garden, Beijing

  Xiaoxiang Courtyard, according to the novel, was planted with slim bamboos, and it used to house Lin Daiyu. The symbolic meaning of the bamboo is in unison with her aloof character. Xiaoxiang has been reminding readers of Ehuang and Nüying who wept until their tears ran dry. It coincided with lachrymose personality of Daiyu.

• 北京大观园内的怡红院

大观园中的每座院子都各有特色。贾宝玉居住的院子名为"怡红院",其名源于院子里的一棵芭蕉和一株海棠,一绿一红,故取名"红香绿玉"。后来因为元春不喜欢其中的"玉",就改名"怡红快绿",简称"怡红院"。

Yihong Courtyard in Grand View Garden, Beijing

Each individual courtyard in the Grand View Garden has its unique feature. The courtyard that Baoyu lived in had its original name Hongxiang Lüyu (fragrant red and green jade), named after a green Chinese banana tree and a red Chinese flowering crabapple in the courtyard. Since Baoyu's elder sister, Yuanchun, didn't like the word "jade", she changed the name to Yihong Kuailü (taking delight in red and green), in short Yihong Courtyard.

群年轻人住了进去。于是这里便有了贾宝玉的怡红院、林黛玉的潇湘馆、薛宝钗的蘅芜苑……

大观园是从贾府中独立出来的一处院所,与外界隔离,是一个理想社会,那么现实中的贾府又是怎样呢?小说中描写的贾府表面上看

her after she entered the imperial palace. After Jia Yuanchun returned to the palace following her family visit, she worried that the garden would fall into disrepair if left unoccupied. Thus, the garden was made at her own request the accommodation of her brother, half-sister, sister-in-law, and cousins. Being

世外桃源

  世外桃源是东晋诗人陶渊明在《桃花源记》中虚构出的一个祥和安乐的世界。文中讲述了这样一个故事：晋朝太元年间，在武陵这个地方有一个渔人。有一天，渔人捕鱼时误入了一个与世隔绝的地方。这里土地平坦，屋舍整齐，有肥沃的田地、美丽的池塘。人们在田里来往耕种，老人和孩子安闲快乐。据他们自己说是他们的祖先为了躲避秦朝的战乱，来到了这里，此后便再也没有出去。他们热情地款待了渔人，并嘱咐他不要将他们的住处说出去。后来，渔人走出了桃花源，等他再去找那个地方，却再也没能找到。现在人们用"世外桃源"这个成语来形容与世隔绝的幽静美好的地方或是幻想中的美好世界。

The Peach Blossom Land

The Peach Blossom Land is a imaginary world created by the poet Tao Yuanming of the Eastern Jin Dynasty in his work *Peach Blossom Spring*, which tells a story about a chance discovery of an ethereal utopia where the people lead an ideal existence in harmony with

- **《桃源图》袁耀（清）**
  此图描绘了东晋陶渊明所写的《桃花源记》的世外桃源。图中突兀的峰岳、如镜的湖水、自在生活其间的人们，无不令人心驰神往。

Peach Blossom Land, by Yuan Yao (Qing Dynasty)
The painting depicted a scene from the *Peach Blossom Land* written by Tao Yuanming of the Eastern Jin Dynasty. Surrounded by lofty mountains and mirror like lakes, people lived there at ease.

nature, unaware of the outside world for centuries. According to the story, a fisherman haphazardly sailed into a river in a forest made up entirely of blossoming peach trees, where even the ground was covered by peach flower petals. When he reached the end of the river, the source turned out to be a grotto. Though narrow at first, he was able to squeeze through and the passage eventually reached a village. The villagers were surprised to see him, but were kind and friendly. They explained that their ancestors escaped to this place during the civil unrest of the Qin Dynasty, and they themselves had not left since or had contact with anyone from the outside. As a result, they had heard nothing of subsequent changes in political regimes. The fisherman was warmly welcmed by the hospitable villagers and stayed for over a week. Upon leaving, he was asked not to reveal this experience to the outside world. However, he marked his route on his way out with signs and later divulged the existence of this idyllic place to others. People of the outside world tried to find it repeatedly, but their attempts were in vain. since then, "Peach Blossom Land" has become a popular Chinese expression, referring to an unexpectedly fantastic place off the beaten path, usually an unspoiled wilderness of great beauty.

娥皇女英的故事

传说娥皇和女英是上古时尧帝的女儿，尧帝晚年把帝位传给了舜，并将两个女儿许配给了他做妻子。有一年，南方发生水灾，舜去实地视察时不幸染病，死于苍梧。娥皇、女英听到舜去世的消息，立即起程赶赴苍梧。等她们到达苍梧时，舜帝已埋在九嶷山下。她们日夜思念着舜帝，眼泪都哭干了，最后哭出了鲜血，血泪滴在碧绿的竹叶上，竹叶立刻染上点点的斑痕。最后，她们二人投湘水而亡，成为湘水之神。她们的事迹也成为历代文人创作的题材。中国伟大诗人屈原《九歌》中的《湘君》《湘夫人》就是最早歌颂二妃的不朽诗篇。

The Story of Ehuang and Nüying

Legend tells that Emperor Yao's daughters Ehuang and Nüying were betrothed to Shun after he gave his throne to Shun. Later, when southern China was affected by floods, Shun went there for inspection and died of illness at Cangwu. Upon their arrival in Cangwu, Ehuang and Nüying found that Emperor Shun was already buried at the foot of Mount Jiuni. They missed him so much that they wept day and night until blood welled out and their tears ran dry, bamboos were tinted with their tears and blood. Finally, they drowned themselves in Xiangjiang River, and became the incarnation of goddess of Xiangjiang River. Their story were portrayed by a number of Chinese Literati. Qu Yuan was the first great Chinese poet to extol Ehuang and Nüying in his poems *Nine Songs*.

- 《九歌图》【局部】张渥（元）

《九歌图》包括屈原像及楚辞《九歌》中的《东皇太一》《云中君》《湘君》《湘夫人》《大司命》《少司命》《东君》《河伯》《山鬼》《国殇》十章内容。

Picture of Nine Songs (Jiu Ge) [Part], by Zhang Wo (Yuan Dynasty)

Picture of Nine Songs is a handscroll painting which includes illustrated poems selected from Qu Yuan's poem series the *Nine Songs* and a portrait of Qu Yuan. The *Nine Songs* actually includes ten articl (or songs): *Donghuang Taiyi* (The Almighty Lord of the East), *Yunzhongjun* (The God of Cloud), *Xiangjun* (The Lord of Xiangjiang River), *Xiangfuren* (The Lady of Xiangjiang River), *Dasiming* (The Great Lord of Fate), *Shaosiming* (The Young Goddess of Fate), *Dongjun* (The God of Sun), *Hebo* (The God of River), *Shangui* (The Goddess of Mountain), *Guoshang* (For Those Fallen for the Country).

- **薛宝钗的蘅芜苑**

  蘅芜是一种香草的名字。薛宝钗居住的蘅芜苑内没有一花一木，只有一些牵藤引蔓的异草仙藤，如蘅芜、藤萝、杜若、薜荔等。这些植物表面无华，暗香浮动，典雅含蓄，与薛宝钗的人物性格十分相符。

  Xue Baochai's Hengwu Courtyard

  Hengwu is a kind of herb. In Xue Baochai's residence, Hengwu Courtyard, there were no flowers or trees, only exotic grasses and vines. These plants appeared plain and unassuming on the surface, yet subtly emitted a delicate fragrance, embodying elegance and gracefulness, which perfectly matched Xue Baochai's personality.

北京大观园

　　在北京西城区南菜园护城河畔，有一座按照曹雪芹《红楼梦》中的大观园建造的实体建筑。它是1984年为拍摄电视剧《红楼梦》而建。全园面积12.5公顷，园内的建筑尽力忠实于原著，再现了文学大师曹雪芹笔下的《红楼梦》官府园林风采。

Grand View Garden in Beijing

A landscape garden was built at Xicheng District, southwest Beijing in 1984 based on the novel using the name of Grand View Garden. The first TV series made based on the novel was filmed in this garden. Covering the area of 12.5 hectares (nearly 32 acres), the garden has been carefully designed to reconstruct Cao Xueqin's Grand View Garden. The most attractive parts are the courtyards, which replicate the residences of the main members of the Jia family.

- 北京大观园
  Grand View Garden in Beijing

● 《全本红楼梦·正堂隆重祭先宗》孙温（清）
Offering Sacrifice to Ancestors, a Scene from A Dream of Red Mansions, by Sun Wen (Qing Dynasty)

是一个繁荣富裕的大家庭，府中的主人们各个温文尔雅，知书识礼，但实际上却是极度腐败，一味骄奢淫逸，最终走向毁灭。

贾府的祖上曾经征战疆场，立下过赫赫战功，但是他们的后代却一个个都是酒囊饭袋。贾敬一味访道炼丹，只求长生不老；贾赦贪恋美色，连母亲身旁的丫鬟都不放过；贾政虽然作风严谨，但是迂腐无能。贾琏作为贾府中的第三代，

very elegant and peaceful, it was a perfect home for Baoyu and the girls. This is how the Yihong Courtyard for Baoyu, Xiaoxiang Courtyard for Daiyu and Hengwu Courtyard for Baochai came to be.

It seemed that Grand View Garden was an ideal place isolated from both Jia's Mansion and the outside world. But what did it look like in reality? As depicted in the novel, on the face of it, Jia's Mansion was a prosperous family with gentle and

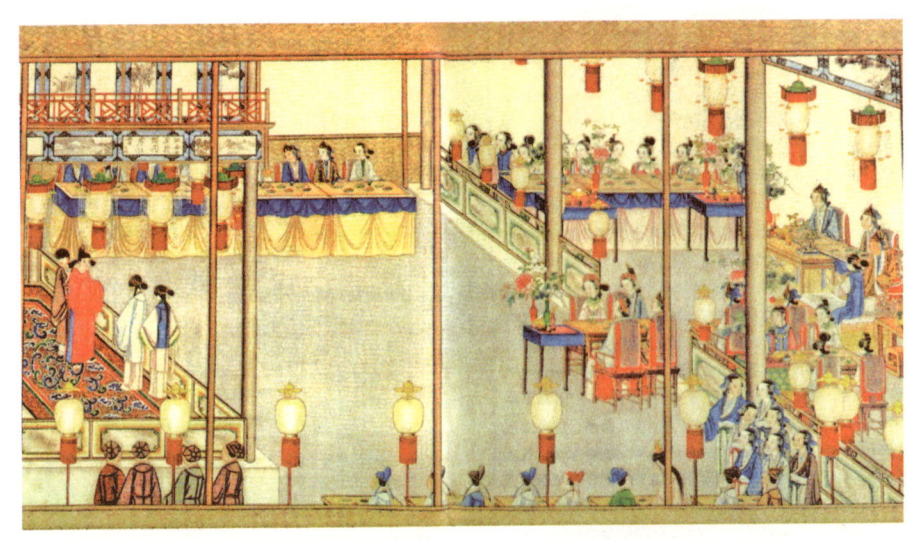

• 《全本红楼梦·荣府花厅开夜宴》孙温（清）
Dinner Party at Flower Hall of Rongguo Mansion, a Scene from
A Dream of Red Mansions, by Sun Wen (Qing Dynasty)

也是人尽皆知的花花太岁。他有一个如花似玉的妻子凤姐，还有一个相貌姣好的侍妾平儿，但这依然满足不了他的色欲。趁凤姐办生日宴会的时机，他与下人偷情，被凤姐发现后告到了贾母那里，贾母却说："什么要紧的事，小孩子们年轻，馋嘴猫儿似的，那里保得住不这么的。"贾母的一番话，道出了这个贵族家庭生活荒淫的真相，也正是这一原因最终葬送了这个大家庭。

此外，贾府在吃穿用度上也十

cultivated people, yet in reality they led an extravagant and dissipated life which accelerated Jia family's decline and bankruptcy.

Jia clan's ancestors have ever established meritorious achievement in battlefield; however, they didn't bequeath their talents to offspring. Members of the later generations were even worse than their elders. Jia Jing, gave up his noble title and devoted the rest of his life to study elixirs, hoping to become an immortal. Jia She, son of Grandmother Jia, was a lecher who fancied beautiful women. Jia Zheng, Baoyu's father and

- **大红猩猩毡盘金彩绣石青妆缎沿边排穗褂子**
这种褂子的下缘有序地排缀着穗状流苏，故称"排穗褂子"。这件衣服所用的布料猩猩毡，是古代一种高级的材质，并且在衣服的领口、袖口、下摆等处还镶上了高级的绸缎。

Scarlet Tasseled Overcoat
This overcoat was made of a high quality felt edged the collar, cuffs of sleeves and the lower hem with satins. The lower hem was tasseled, hence its name.

分奢华。一道名为"茄鲞"的菜肴需要十来只鸡来配；一顿螃蟹宴更是够庄稼人过上一年的。在服饰上，贾府的丫鬟都穿的与普通人家不同，府中的主人更是穿金戴银。小说中提到宝玉曾经有一件俄罗斯国的孔雀毛做的氅衣，一不小心烧了个洞，缝补时使用的是金线。作者正是通过对这一大家庭日常生活的描写来暴露现实社会中豪贵家族的腐朽和罪恶。

the younger son of Grandmother Jia, was a disciplinarian, yet pedantic and incompetant. Jia Lian, as the third generation of Jia clan, was also a notorious womanizer. He had a beautiful wife and had an affair with a good-looking maid, but he was not contended. He even had an affair on the occasion of his wife's birthday banquet. Having found it, his wife Wang Xifeng reported it to Grandmother Jia, who replied, "It is not big deal. You can't blame the young for being tempted." Her words reflected the dissoluteness of this noble family, which eventually led to the downfall of it.

Their extravagant way of life has been infiltrated into every aspect of their daily life. A dish of eggplant "Qiexiang" has to be served with a dozen of chickens; the value of a crab feast amounted to one year's expenditure of a common family; the costumes for maids

在《红楼梦》的艺术世界里，一种末世的苍凉意味无时无刻不笼罩着整部小说。正如《红楼梦》第一回中的一首《好了歌》所写：

世人都晓神仙好，惟有功名忘不了！
古今将相在何方？荒冢一堆草没了。
世人都晓神仙好，只有金银忘不了！
终朝只恨聚无多，及到多时眼闭了。

- 《红楼梦粉本·双玉听琴》

Baoyu and Miaoyu Appreciating the Music Scene a from *A Dream of Red Mansions*

贾宝玉和栊翠庵的尼姑妙玉经过林黛玉的潇湘馆时，听到黛玉在抚琴，便静静地坐在潇湘馆外的石头上听琴。

When Baoyu and Miaoyu, a young nun from Buddhist cloisters of the Rongguo Mansion, passed by Xiaoxiang Courtyard where Daiyu lived, they were enchanted by the music, so they sat on a stone outside of her Courtyard to enjoy it.

and servants of Jia family were much better than what the ordinary people wore, let alone the masters. As mentioned in the novel, Baoyu had a Russian-made overcoat made of peacock feather, and his maid mended a burnt hole on it with gold thread. Detailed and vivid depictions of the aristocrat's daily life revealed social injustice and corruption of the time.

An eschatological sense casted a deep gloom over the novel. As *All Good Things Must End* chanted in Chapter 1:

"All men long to be immortals
Yet to riches and fame each aspires;
The great ones of the past, where are they now?
Their graves are a mass of briars.
All men long to be immortals,
Yet silver and gold they prize
And grub for money all their lives
Till death seals up their eyes.
All men long to be immortals
Yet dote on the wives they've wed,
Who swear to love their husband evermore
But remarry as soon as he's dead.
All men long to be immortals
Yet with getting sons won't have done.
Although fond parents are legion,
Who ever saw a really filial son?"

世人都晓神仙好，只有娇妻忘不了！
君生日日说恩情，君死又随人去了。
世人都晓神仙好，只有儿孙忘不了！
痴心父母古来多，孝顺子孙谁见了？

明确地道出了"人生到头来，都是为他人作嫁衣裳"的悲观厌世情怀。

《红楼梦》的伟大，除了它叙述了一个大家庭从兴盛到衰亡的过程，还在于它描写了贾府中众多年轻女子的凄美爱情，其中尤以贾宝玉和林黛玉之间的爱情最为凄美、缠绵。

贾宝玉和林黛玉之间的爱情是有着前世宿因的。《红楼梦》的作者在第一回便讲述了绛珠仙草还泪神瑛侍者的神话故事：传说西方灵河岸的三生石畔有一株绛珠草，由于神瑛侍者每日用甘露浇灌，后来这株草变幻化成了人形。有一天，神英侍者想到人间经历一番，绛珠草因一直想回报神瑛侍者的灌溉之恩，便决定追随他也到人间走一遭。绛珠草曾说："他是甘露之惠，我并无此水可还。……但把我一生所有的眼泪还他，也偿还得过他了。"神瑛侍者便是贾宝玉，绛珠草便是林黛玉。作者在小说的开篇便讲述这样一个

• 《红楼梦图咏·黛玉》改琦（清）
Portrait of Daiyu, by Gai Qi (Qing Dynasty)

It clearly expresses the pessimistic view that "One's life is spent laboring in vain, only to benefit others in the end".

A Dream of Red Mansions has been seen as a masterpiece because it depicted not only the rise and fall of the feudal families of that era but also the charming and woeful love stories that took place in Jia's Mansion, especially the love between Baoyu and Daiyu.

The love between Baoyu and Daiyu in this life was predestined. As a fairy tales goes in Chapter 1, on the bank of

故事，既阐明了贾宝玉、林黛玉爱情故事的前世宿因，又暗指这不是寻常的爱情故事，而是一幕以"还泪"的方式写出"儿女之真情"的凄美爱情悲剧。

林黛玉与贾宝玉从小一起长大，青梅竹马，志同道合。他们都对为官从政之道不感兴趣。当有人劝宝玉好好读书以考取功名时，宝玉却说："林姑娘从来说过这些混账话不曾？若他也说过这些混账

the Sacred River in the west, beside the Stone of Three Incarnations there grew a Vermilion Pearl Plant which was watered every day with sweet dew by the attendant Shen Ying. As months and years went by, the Vermilion Pearl Plant cast off its plant nature and took human form. One day Shen Ying decided to visit the world of men. It was a chance for Vermilion Pearl Plant to repay her debt of gratitude. She has ever wanted to say, "He gives me sweet dew, but I have no water to repay his kindness. I shall repay him with as many tears as I can shed in a lifetime, and I may be able to clear this debt." Daiyu was the Vermilion Pearl Plant in her previous incarnation, while Baoyu was the attendant Shen Ying. Such a tale as "repaying kindness with tears"

- 江苏南京红楼艺文苑内的宝黛读西厢塑像

  《西厢记》是一部中国古代爱情小说，在当时是闺中的禁书。但是贾宝玉、林黛玉两人却一起在树下看西厢，共同沉浸在唯美的爱情故事中。

  Statues of Baoyu and Daiyu in Red Mansions Literature and Art Garden, Nanjing, Jiangsu Province Depicting a Scene of Reading *The Romance of the Western Bower*

  The Romance of the Western Bower was an officially banned book during old times, yet Baoyu and Daiyu read it under the tree immersing in sweet love stories.

话，我早和他生分了。"

　　虽然贾宝玉与林黛玉之间有着牢固的爱情基础，但是在强大的家族利益面前他们的爱情还是脆弱的。在王熙凤的精心策划下，趁宝玉糊涂之际让宝钗冒充黛玉和宝玉成亲，酿成了黛玉在宝玉新婚之夜泪尽而逝、宝玉出家为僧、宝钗年轻守寡的爱情和婚姻悲剧。

has hinted that their predestined, unusual love was doomed to be a tragedy.

　　Daiyu and Baoyu grew up together, and they were like-minded. Both of them had no interest in an official or political career. When someone persuaded him to study hard to get an official job, he replied, "Daiyu has never said such impudent remark; otherwise, I will brush her off."

　　Even though their relationship had a solid foundation, they were forced to give way to the interest of feudal family, ending with love and marriage tragedies. Baoyu walked into Wang Xifeng's elaborately planed trap, conceived of marrying Daiyu, who were pretended by Baochai. On his wedding day, Daiyu

● **珐琅彩龙凤纹双联瓶（清）**
在中国传统观念中，龙和凤代表着吉祥如意，龙凤连用寓意喜庆之事。

The Porcelain Enamel Siamesed Vase with the Pattern of Colored Loong and Phoenix (Qing Dynasty)
Loong and phoenix symbolize good luck and happiness in Chinese tradition, hence the patterns on this vase.

- 《红楼梦》绣像
  The Tapestry Portrait of *A Dream of Red Mansions*

除了贾宝玉、林黛玉之间的凄美爱情，尤三姐与柳湘莲的爱情在《红楼梦》中也显得格外耀眼。尤三姐是贾珍妻子尤氏的继母带来的妹妹。因为姐姐的原因，她也住在贾府里。尤三姐不仅相貌长得漂亮，而且性格刚烈。贾府中的一些好色之徒曾经对她有所企图，但是都被她狠狠地回绝了。

abandoned herself to grief and died. Later, Baoyu became a monk, leaving Baochai in widowhood.

The love story between Third Sister You and Liu Xianglian was also highlighted in *A Dream of Red Mansions*. She lived with her elder sister, Jia Zhen's wife, in Jia's Mansion. Many womanizers in Jia's Mansion had an eye to her beauty. But she was so strong-minded that she rejected them bluntly.

Liu Xianglian was an orphaned son of a noble family. He was a good-looking man and enjoyed playing spear and sticks. Therefore, after his parent's died, he often played a part in a professional opera performance, where Third Sister You and Liu Xianglian fell in love at first sight. Since then, she vowed to marry Liu Xianglian. Upon leaining this, Liu Xianglian had someone take a sword out of a pair to Third Sister You as a token of love. Third Sister You was delighted to see the sword, and further strengthened her resolve to marry him.

- 尤三姐像

  Portrait of Third Sister You

● 柳湘莲像
Portrait of Liu Xianglian

柳湘莲原是世家子弟，但父母双亡后便漂泊四方。他性格豪爽，喜欢舞枪弄棒，由于长相俊美，经常在戏曲表演中客串一些角色。尤三姐便是在柳湘莲的一次演出中与他一见钟情，之后便发誓非柳湘莲不嫁。后来，有人将此事转告给了柳湘莲，他便托那人将一把鸳鸯宝剑作为定情信物带给了尤三姐。尤三姐见到宝剑后十分高兴，更加坚定了自己的想法。

几个月之后，柳湘莲进京见到了贾宝玉，贾宝玉便将尤三姐的身世经历告诉了他。当柳湘莲听说尤三姐是住在贾府中的，便决定要回鸳鸯剑。因为在他看来，贾府中的人都是不干净的，尤三姐也不会例外。当尤三姐听说柳湘莲悔婚后，觉得他不了解自己的真心，便从床上摘

In a few months, Liu Xianglian came to the capital and met Baoyu, who told him the story about Third Sister You. Knowing that she lived in Jia's Mansion, he decided to take back his sword and broke his betrothal to Third Sister You because he disliked members of the Jia family, and he wanted to have no

● 《红楼梦》绣像
The Tapestry Portrait of *A Dream of Red Mansions*

下鸳鸯剑，自刎身亡。这时候，柳湘莲才知道尤三姐是清白的，但是为时已晚，一对有情人就这样因误会而成憾。

在《红楼梦》中，作者通过描写这些勇于追求自己幸福的年轻男女来宣扬一种新的爱情观念，具有非常超前的意识。

association with them. Not until Third Sister You committed suicide with Liu's swords in front of him did he understand her sincerity, yet it was too late. Such pair of lovers had a regretful ending caused by misunderstanding.

In *A Dream of Red Mansions,* the author promotes a progressive view of love by depicting these young men and women who courageously pursue their own happiness.

曹雪芹纪念馆

　　曹雪芹纪念馆位于西山脚下的北京植物园内，是一组被低矮院墙环绕着的长方形仿清建筑。1971年，人们在香山地区正白旗村发现一座带有几组题壁诗的老式民居，后经专家鉴定是曹雪芹著书之所，后以此为基础建成了该纪念馆。

　　展馆前后两排共18间房舍。前排展室陈列有清代旗人的生活环境，曹雪芹在西山的生活、创作环境的模型，200年来有关曹雪芹身世的重大发现，及有关文章、书籍。后排房屋的展示内容为曹雪芹的生平家世、《红楼梦》的影响两个部分。展品中有再现曹雪芹时代民风民俗的八仙桌、躺柜墩箱、青花瓷器，以及《红楼梦》中提到的一些民俗器物如银锁、手炉、拂尘等。此外，纪念馆还另辟专室展出对曹雪芹研究的成果及各种版本的《红楼梦》。

Cao Xueqin Memorial Museum

Cao Xueqin Memorial Museum, a Qing-dynasty-style construction surrounded by low courtyard walls, is located in Beijing Botanical Garden at the foot of Western Hills. In 1971, Some discovered an old style folk house in a village in Beijing, with walls inscribed with poems. According to experts, it was Cao Xueqin's dwelling where he wrote *A Dream of Red Mansions*. Thereafter, museum in memory of Cao Xueqin was built on site.

　　The Musenm has 18 rooms in two rows. The front

- 北京曹雪芹纪念馆内的曹雪芹塑像
Statue of Cao Xueqin in Cao Xueqin Memorial Museum, Beijing

row exhibits models of the living conditions of the Eight Banners in the Qing Dynasty, Cao Xueqin's living and composing conditions, and some discoveries and related books and articles about Cao Xueqin's background. There are two major topics shown in the back row of the rooms; one is related to Cao Xueqin's parentage and life experiences, the other related to his masterpiece. The exhibits include items that recreate the customs and traditions of Cao Xueqin's era, such as the "eight-immortal" tables, storage cabinets, and blue-and-white porcelain. Additionally, there are household items mentioned in *A Dream of Red Mansions*. The memorial hall also features a dedicated room showcasing the achievements of Redology research and various editions of *A Dream of Red Mansions*.

- 警幻仙曲演红楼梦
  The Goddess of Disenchantment Expounds *A Dream of Red Mansion*